Lily Quench

and the Treasure of Mote Ely

Lily Quench

and the Treasure of Mote Ely

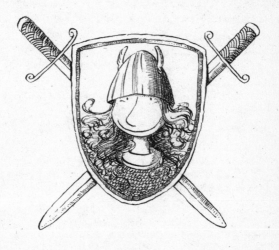

NATALIE JANE PRIOR

Illustrations by Janine Dawson

PUFFIN BOOKS

For Elena

PUFFIN BOOKS
Published by Penguin Group
Penguin Young Readers Group,
345 Hudson Street, New York, New York 10014, U.S.A.
Penguin Books Ltd, 80 Strand, London WC2R ORL, England
Penguin Books Australia Ltd, 250 Camberwell Road,
Camberwell, Victoria 3124, Australia
Penguin Books Canada Ltd, 10 Alcorn Avenue, Toronto, Ontario, Canada M4V 3B2
Penguin Books (N.Z.) Ltd, 182-190 Wairau Road, Auckland 10, New Zealand

First published in Australia and New Zealand by Hodder Headline Australia Pty
Limited, a member of the Hodder Headline Group, 2002
Published by Puffin Books, a division of Penguin Young Readers Group, 2004

1   3   5   7   9   10   8   6   4   2

Text copyright © Natalie Jane Prior, 2002
Illustrations copyright © Janine Dawson, 2002
All rights reserved

LIBRARY OF CONGRESS CATALOGING-IN-PUBLICATION DATA

Prior, Natalie Jane, 1963-
Lily Quench and the treasure of Mote Ely /Natalie Jane Prior;
illustrations by Janine Dawson.
p. cm.
Summary: Kidnapped and taken into the past to a creepy,
crumbling castle, Lily Quench searches for the long-lost
treasure of Mote Ely—and a way back into her own time.
ISBN 0-14-240022-X
[Dragons—Fiction. 2. Time travel—Fiction. 3. Buried treasure—Fiction. 4. Fantasy.]
I. Dawson, Janine, ill. II. Title.
PZ7.P9373Lm 2004
[Fic]—dc22   2003058431

Puffin Books ISBN 0-14-240022-X
Printed in the United States of America

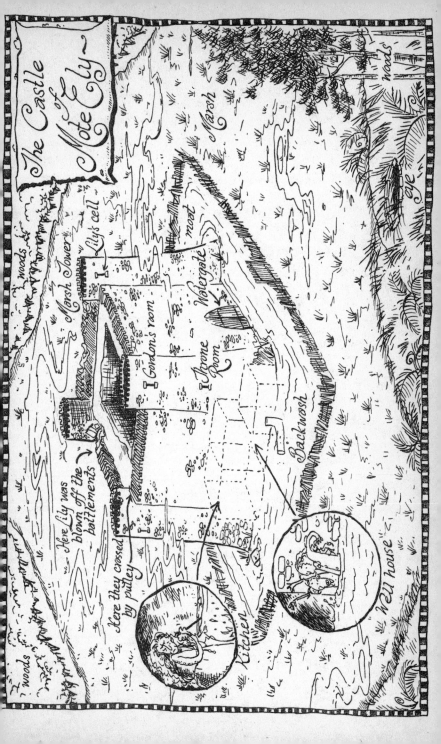

chapter one

The Eye in the Grass

The skies over the Island of Skansey were clear and blue, and Lily Quench was on Merryweather Hill above her apple orchard, eagerly scanning the horizon for signs of an approaching dragon. Her friends, King Lionel and Queen Evangeline of Ashby, were coming to visit. Lily had swept her cottage in readiness and made a cake and some scones; she had changed the bed and been up into the apple loft above her bedroom to find the best, shiniest red apples from last autumn's crop. Then she had gone up onto the hill to watch for her royal visitors' arrival. Queen Dragon had promised to be back in time for afternoon tea, so she expected them to appear at any moment.

Lily made some daisy chains and sat in the long grass, looking out peacefully over the island. She could see her little red cottage among the apple trees at the foot of the hill, the beach in the cove where Queen Dragon liked to land, and her sheep grazing placidly in the soft green grass. A few miles away across the water she could see the volcano where Queen Dragon slept in a cavern under a crater full of boiling mud. Today, a few puffs of smoke floated up from it, but they were so wispy they might have been baby clouds. Lily looked up into the sky, saw a small crimson dot silhouetted against the afternoon sun, and jumped to her feet. If she hurried, she would just have time to put the kettle on before her visitors arrived.

Lily started running down the hill, but she had scarcely gone a dozen steps when she put her foot down in a patch of fern and felt it skid into nothingness. With a shocked yell, she pitched forward and thudded to the ground.

"Oooof!"

Lily rolled over and sat up. Nearby, what appeared to be a rabbit hole yawned in the middle of a patch of broken fern fronds. It looked uncannily like an eye surrounded by green eyelashes. Lily crawled gingerly back to it and parted the ferns. The hole was actually much bigger than she had originally thought, and an ancient rim of bricks still showed in places through the mud, like the coping at the top of a well shaft. Her foot had just caught the edge. A step or two to the left and she might have disappeared completely.

"What a strange place for a well." Lily looked around for some sign of a ruined house or building that might once have used it. Her cottage had its own well at the back door, and she could not imagine why anyone would want to climb all the way up the hill for water. Suddenly, a funny smell floated up the well shaft: a dank smell, like a marsh or bog. Lily recoiled and shivered, as if she were suddenly cold.

She looked up. As usual, the sky was blue. There were swallows and a few white clouds, like lamb's tails. In the distance she could see her sheep moving slowly about the fields. But there was definitely a strange shift in the air, a feeling as if it was about to rain.

"How peculiar." Once more, Lily examined the crumbling brickwork. It was plainly very, very old—the bricks were reddish brown and the same odd narrow shape as the ones in the oldest part of Ashby Castle. A strange itch, like the prickle of pins and needles, started up in Lily's left elbow. Anybody else would probably have ignored it. But Lily was a Quench, born of an ancient line of dragon slayers and adventurers, and the tiny patch of scaly dragon skin on her arm was like a magical barometer that warned her of approaching danger.

Her visitors forgotten, Lily bent aside the ferns that fringed the edge of the well and started scraping the dirt away from the brickwork. At this point she received a second shock.

The well had eyelashes carved into the stone.

A crumbling path led down Merryweather Hill, but petered out only a little distance away under the grass. Once, people must have used it to come to the well, and something told Lily they had not been looking for water. On impulse, she leaned over the edge and peered in. She could not see anything, but the strange, dank smell swelled and grew stronger until it made the hairs lift on the back of her neck. Then, suddenly, her elbow started tingling so hard it hurt.

Stagnant water started rushing up the well, or Lily herself went rushing down to meet it, she did not know which. She felt a blast of cold air streaming over her face and saw a face she recognized. It was older than when she had last seen it in the snow and ice of the Black Mountains, and the expression was harder, but there was no doubt who it was.

The boy at the bottom of the well looked up, and Lily knew he had seen her, too. He started saying something she could not hear, and then he reached out his hand. Lily reached hers out, too. She shouted his name, *"Gordon!"* and the sound went echoing down the well. A tremendous pulling sensation gripped her, as if something or someone was urging her to jump into the well. Lily grabbed hold of the brickwork, and then the magic inexplicably faltered. Gordon dropped his hand and turned away, the pull slackened and his face started disappearing, as if a dark veil was being pulled across it.

Lily struggled to hold on to him. "Gordon! Come back!"

"No, Lily." This time his voice came through to her clearly. "I want you to come to me."

Lily fell back with a thump on the hard ground at the well's edge, and fainted.

chapter two

Attack in the Dark

Tick, tock, tick, tock, tick tock. The sound of a clock ticking echoed around inside Lily's head. She sighed and wrinkled her nose. A familiar smell of fresh apples tickled her nostrils, and she blinked and opened her eyes.

"Hello, Lily," said a voice. "Are you feeling any better?"

"Y-your Majesty!" Lily sat up, and for a moment the whole room went wobbly. King Lionel—for the voice was his—reached over to steady her. Gradually Lily's eyes focused and she realized she was in her own bedroom in her cottage at the foot of the hill.

The door opened. "Hello, Lily," said Queen Evangeline. She was expecting a baby and was much fatter than the last time Lily had seen her. "You look better. I've just made a pot of tea. If you're feeling up to it, Queen Dragon is waiting for us in the garden."

"I'm fine. That'd be lovely." Lily waited while the king and queen left the room, then hastily climbed out of bed and pulled on her shoes. She went outside and found her friends sitting under the apple trees, near a small patch of blue lilies growing in the dappled shade.

A blanket was spread out under the trees with a picnic tea. Evangeline was swinging lazily under the apples in Lily's hammock, and Queen Dragon was munching on some old refrigerators she had picked up from her stockpile on the beach. When she saw Lily, a fridge door went down the wrong way and she almost choked.

"Lily. Are you feeling all right?" A few wisps of smoke came puffing from her nostrils, and her huge yellow eyes were round with concern.

"I'm much better, Queen Dragon. Honestly."

Lily sat down and started pouring cups of tea, hoping none of her visitors could see how shaky her hand was. Meanwhile, Evangeline stepped off the hammock. She cut up the buttered tea cake, and Lionel handed around the plates.

"Delicious scones, Lily," he said, and for the next few minutes there was silence as everyone began to eat. Lily had two scones and a piece of cake, but they tasted dry and crumbly in her mouth. She knew her friends must be wondering what had made her faint on the hillside, but they were too polite to ask.

In the end, she decided to say something. "Something really strange happened to me this afternoon," she began. "I was out on Merry-weather Hill, and I almost fell into a well. I had the strangest feeling, like I was being sucked down into it. And I saw a face in the water. That was when I fainted."

"Did you recognize who it was?" asked Evangeline.

Lily nodded reluctantly. "It was Gordon."

"That's bad news," said Lionel gravely. "When Gordon's father died, I'd hoped we'd heard the last of the Black Counts. Ever since General Sark took over the Black Empire, things in Ashby have been quiet. It looked like we might be safe for a while. But if Gordon's out there, sooner or later he's going to want to claim his father's empire." For a moment, Lionel brooded silently and Lily knew he was remembering his own long years of hiding, working as the Ashby Castle librarian and plotting to drive out the invaders who had stolen his throne. She knew Lionel could understand how Gordon felt. When at last the king spoke again, it was on another subject entirely.

"I suppose I ought to tell you why Evangeline and I have come to visit. We've had some rather strange news. Have you ever heard of Mote Ely?"

"I don't think so," said Lily. "Is it a person or a place?"

"It's a castle," said Lionel. "A ruined castle in the marshes at the foot of the Black Mountains. It was built hundreds of years ago in the time of Mad Brian Quench, but the climate was unhealthy. The owners soon deserted it, and the castle fell into a ruin."

"I'd never heard of it either," put in Evangeline.

"What about you, Queen Dragon?"

"Well, the name does ring a bell," Queen Dragon admitted. "The problem is, I've raided so many castles over the centuries, I can't remember half of them."

"You might remember this one," said Evangeline. "It's supposed to be haunted by the ghost of Lily's ancestor, Matilda Drakescourge. Some woodcutters claim to have seen her in the nearby forest."

"Haunted!" Queen Dragon sat up and looked alarmed. Lily patted her scaly leg.

"Don't worry, Queen Dragon. There's no such thing as ghosts. My grandmother, Ursula, told me so when I visited the Singing Wood, and she's dead, so she ought to know."

"In that case, you won't mind investigating," said Lionel.

"I suppose not," Lily said a little doubtfully. "If you think it's really important."

"If you ask me, it's totally unimportant," said Queen Dragon. "Who cares if old Crater Face is haunting some tumbledown castle at the back of beyond, when that boy Gordon's likely to come back at any moment? Don't you realize? If there's an Eye Stone on Skansey, we could all be in terrible danger."

"An Eye Stone?" asked Lionel. "What's that, Queen Dragon?"

"It's a magical gateway, a way of traveling quickly between one place and time and another," explained Queen Dragon. "Remember how Gordon disappeared through that stone in the Black Mountains a few months ago? The well Lily found this afternoon works the same way. Nobody knows who originally made them, but they're quite ancient. If a magic's made strong enough, it can last a very long time."

"Maybe we should find out more," suggested Evangeline. "They sound like they could be useful."

"Useful?" Queen Dragon snorted. "I suppose they would be useful, if you could control them. No doubt the magic worked for whoever built the things, but the Eyes have a nasty habit of dumping other travelers where and when they don't plan to go. I wouldn't use one, no matter how desperate I was. They're bad magic and bad news. In fact, I think we should try and find a way of closing off the Eye Lily found this afternoon. Otherwise it won't be safe for her to stay here. Old Crater Face's ghost will have to wait."

"Poor Matilda Drakescourge," said Evangeline.

"She wasn't 'Poor Matilda Drakescourge' when she threw a bottle of Quenching Drops at my friend, Serpentine Bridgestock," said Queen Dragon darkly.

They talked things over a little longer, until the sun started dropping and the light went. Then Queen Dragon flew back to her volcano for a more substantial dinner and Lily lit the lamps in the cottage and cooked a human meal with homegrown peas, baby potatoes, and three small fish she had caught in the sea that morning. After they had eaten, the king and queen said good night and went to bed in Lily's room. Lily herself fetched her blanket and pillow and went outside to sleep in her hammock under the stars.

The hammock hung from the oldest of the apple trees in her orchard. On fine days, Lily liked to lie there with a book and maybe an apple or two to crunch on, and look up at the clouds scudding silently across the sky. Tonight there were no clouds, just stars to gaze at through the apple boughs, and a low sliver of moon hanging over the sea. Lily adjusted the pillow under her head and wriggled until she was comfortable under her blue crocheted coverlet. The hammock swayed gently back and forth, and, to the sound of crickets chirping, she drifted off to sleep.

In her dreams, she found herself in the Black Mountains again. Gordon was there, too, and this time he looked the way he had when she had first met him: a small, serious boy with a pale face and black hair. They were standing together on top of Dragon's Downfall, looking over the icy cliff where Gordon's father, the Black Count, had fallen to his frightful death. Gordon was crying, and his hot tears melted the snow they were standing on. Lily could feel the ice start to shift under her feet. "Stop it!" she cried, "stop it!" But Gordon only cried the harder, until all at once the cliff collapsed beneath them with a mighty roar, and they were both thrown headlong into the icy abyss.

Lily felt her stomach clutch with fear. As she started to fall, her eyes suddenly opened and she realized she was awake.

"Watch out!" said a girl's voice. Before Lily had

a chance to do anything, someone threw her crocheted blanket over her face and tipped her out of the hammock onto the ground.

Rough hands bundled her up and started carrying her away. Terrified, Lily smelled hot, sweaty bodies crowding close around her and heard her captors panting. She struggled and shouted, but the blanket muffled her cries and then somebody walloped her hard and knocked all the wind out of her. Lily stopped shouting. The cottage was too far away for Lionel and Evangeline to hear her anyway. There had to be another way of warning them about what was happening.

The red bead bracelet that she had put on in honor of the royal visit pressed hard against her wrist. It had been a Christmas present from the king and queen, and the individual beads spelled out her name. Lily rolled the bracelet off and snapped the elastic. The beads slipped into her palm and she poked one through a hole in the crocheted blanket and let it fall.

Her captors were going uphill now, grumbling about how heavy she was. There were several boys and the sharp-voiced girl, whom the others called Veronica. Lily concentrated on dropping her beads one by one, and then suddenly her captors dumped her unceremoniously on the ground. Lily fought to free herself from her coverings, but before she could throw off the blanket somebody gave her a vicious push. For a split second, Lily felt herself teeter on the edge of nothingness. Then she toppled over the brink and plunged headfirst into darkness.

chapter three
Kidnapped

Lily screamed with terror. The thin sound of her voice streamed in her wake as she fell down the well shaft, and behind her she could hear whoops and cries as her captors jumped in after her. The crocheted blanket came away from her face and she realized she was shooting down a long dark tunnel with walls that gleamed like glass. It was a bit like the coldest, fastest ride she had ever been on in her life.

For a minute or more Lily whizzed silently onward. It seemed as if she were going nowhere, and then a pale glimmer of light suddenly appeared ahead of her. Lily rushed toward it, screaming. A second later, she shot out of a hole like a crater and landed with a thud on a flat, squelchy piece of ground.

Lily sat up. Water started soaking immediately through her dress, and she felt mud ooze beneath her bare toes. Then she heard a voice behind her. "Watch out!" it shouted. Lily moved hastily out of the way, just as a boy with big boots and a pale freckled face came shooting out of the crater. He was followed rapidly by a girl with dark, raggedly cut hair, and several other boys, all in shabby and extremely dirty clothes.

Lily scrambled to her feet, but realized there was nowhere for her to run to. She was surrounded by strangers, in a bleak and desolate bit of wasteland. Behind her, at a little distance, was a wood with thick stands of trees, but around the crater was only mud and marsh and mist. Tufts of grass poked up through stagnant puddles, and a big clump of rushes grew close to the water. Lily's crocheted blanket was still lying on the ground near her feet. Before she had a chance to do anything about it, the girl, Veronica, bent down and picked it up.

"That's nice," she said approvingly. "I'll have that for my bunk back at the castle. Murdo! Get the boats. We've wasted enough time already. The general will be waiting."

Murdo was the boy with the boots. He snapped an order, and two of the other boys disappeared into the bulrushes and returned in a minute, pulling a flat-bottomed skiff through the squelchy marsh mud. There was one red bead left in Lily's hand. She dropped it into the mud and, trying hard not to look as scared as she felt, let her captors bundle her roughly into the boat.

Veronica turned up the wick on the lantern she was carrying and climbed into the skiff with Lily, Murdo, and two other boys. The rest scratched around in the rushes, eventually turning out some battered coracles that they carried to the water's edge. Lily heard someone grumbling loudly that his coracle was full of water. Then the skiff was pushed off into the shallow waters of the marsh, and they floated away.

Lily sat in the middle of the boat, shivering with cold. Veronica, who was already much more warmly dressed than she was, now draped the crocheted blanket around her own shoulders as if her prisoner's comfort hardly mattered to her. Lily glumly realized that it probably didn't. The little lantern burned in the bows of the skiff, and there was moonglow behind a cloud, but otherwise it was completely dark. Lily could hear the soft plunk of poles in the water as the two boys who had accompanied them poled the skiff along, and the splash of paddles as the coracles followed. Clumps of marsh grass stood up like miniature islands in the mist, but the farther they went into the deeper water, the fewer they became. At last, after about ten minutes, Lily spied the dark bulk of a building ahead of them. Then their skiff came to an abrupt halt in front of what looked like a fence. Murdo stood up to unhook a narrow gate. As they poled through, Lily saw that it was a palisade of sharp sticks, poking up out of the water. They had left the marsh and entered an artificial waterway.

The water inside the gate was still and stagnant. It smelled horrible, even worse than the marsh smell, like school toilets nobody ever flushed. Lily gagged, but the others didn't seem to care or notice. Now that they were coming up close to the building, Lily realized apprehensively that it was a huge castle with blackened stone walls, rising up out of the marshland. At the foot of the walls, the skiff stopped. Lily saw someone moving on the battlements, and then a girl's voice called out sternly, "You, on the lake. Friend or foe?"

Veronica spoke in a clear, loud voice. "Friend."

"Is that you, Major Veronica?" called the girl. "What's the watchword?"

"'Victory over Ashby,'" Veronica called back. There was a creaking sound, and a gate rose slowly in the castle wall. Lily caught a brief glimpse of two more boys, operating a winch as their skiff was poled silently through, and then they were inside the castle and drawing up to a small wharf, with the coracles pulling in behind them, one by one.

"Tell the general we've arrived, Gibber," said Veronica, and one of the boys got out and obediently ran off. Veronica and Murdo climbed out of the skiff and hoisted Lily out. She jumped awkwardly onto wet, slippery stonework. Her captors led her up a winding flight of stairs into a castle bailey, a huge enclosed space with towering walls. Unlike Ashby Castle, which was a friendly place with its flower beds and the faded royal flags snapping cheerfully atop its turrets, this castle was gloomy and damp. A big fire burned in a shallow pit in the center of the open space, and several boys and girls were huddled around it. The night air was chillier than ever, and the mist rising from the moat seemed to press like ghostly fingers against Lily's hair and skin.

Lily followed Murdo and Veronica through a door at the foot of a tall tower. They went up some more stairs and on the first floor stopped at a stout wooden door. Veronica's knock was answered by a stern-looking boy in a red-and-blue-striped jacket.

"Come in," he said. "The general is expecting you," and the next thing Lily knew she was inside the room and standing in front of a carved, thronelike chair. A few lean, mean-looking boys and girls were lounging about, and a fire burned and smoked on an enormous hearth. At that exact moment an inner door opened and another boy came into the room. Everyone jumped to their feet and snapped to attention. Lily felt a tremendous pang of fear.

"At ease, soldiers." Gordon sat down on his

throne and folded his hands over its carved armrests. He was dressed in a plain dark suit that was much neater than anything anyone else was wearing, and there was a strip of gold braid around his collar. His face was very pale and stern-looking. Lily thought he looked a lot older than when she had last seen him in the Black Mountains a few months before. Then, Gordon had been just a spoiled brat who happened to be the only son of the most powerful man in the world. He had been selfish, bad-tempered, and untrustworthy, yet he had still helped her escape from the Black Citadel, even though she was his enemy. In a funny way, Lily had liked him and been sorry for what had happened to him.

On that last dreadful day in the Black Mountains, Gordon had lost his home, his father, and his empire. He had flung himself through the Eye Stone, screaming, and disappeared. Nobody had known where or when he had ended up, or even if he was still alive. Now that she had found him again, Lily was not sure she liked the change the last few months had made.

Veronica went over and whispered in Gordon's ear. He listened carefully, then turned to Lily and said, "Hello, Lily. I suppose it must come as a bit of a shock, finding me here. How's that dragon friend of yours? Still around?"

"Queen Dragon is well," said Lily, trying to sound brave. "By now, she's probably wondering what's happened to me."

"She can wonder for all she's worth, then," said Gordon unpleasantly. "So, tell me. How long has it been in your time since you saw me?"

At first, Lily did not understand the question. Then she looked at Gordon again and realized what he meant. For him, here on the other side of the Eye Stone, much more time had passed than had for her. That was how he'd had enough time to put together his gang of lean, rough boys and girls—and why he looked so much older than he had the last time Lily had seen him.

"It's been a—while." Lily had been going to say, "a few months," but Lionel's warning about Gordon coming back to claim his empire made her suddenly think there was more behind the question than there seemed. "Ages. It's been ages. Everyone's completely forgotten you."

Murdo smirked, and Gordon looked annoyed. "They'll remember me soon enough. Still, there's plenty of time to talk about that later. As you can see, I'm in charge here. Let me introduce you to my senior officers. This is Major Veronica. She's my deputy, looks after the troops, and helps with strategy. And this is Captain Murdo. He's in charge of security and special projects and will be looking after you while you're staying here." He gave Lily a searching look. "And now, I think it's time for you to rest. We've a guest room prepared for you in the Marsh Tower. Murdo will take you there. The rest of you are dismissed. Hang on, Rabbit. Not you. Come back. I've got a job for you."

A small boy with pale hair, freckles, and sticking-out teeth came forward out of a corner.

"Rabbit," said Gordon, "this is Lily Quench. Go to Aunt Cassy and get her some supper. Then take it to the Marsh Tower. Do you understand?"

The boy nodded.

Veronica looked annoyed. "Don't nod, you idiot. Salute. How many times do I have to tell you?"

"Sorry, Major Veronica." The boy saluted, cringing, and scuttled off.

Lily turned to Murdo. "If you're looking after

me, do you think you could find me some warm clothes? I'm freezing."

"I'll see what I can do," said Murdo. "But I won't make any promises. We're short of a lot of things here." He snapped his fingers, and a slightly older boy got up from the fire. He fell in behind Murdo and followed him and Lily back downstairs and across the bailey to a crumbling tower on the northern edge of the keep.

Murdo unlocked a door. Lily was marched up some winding stairs to the very top of the tower. It was such a long way that by the time they reached a stout wooden door, she was positively dizzy. She had hardly paused to catch her breath when a hand from behind gave her a rough shove in the middle of her back. Lily stumbled forward into darkness, and the door closed behind her. Then she heard the key turning in the lock, and the guard settling down at his post, and she realized that it was only a prison after all.

chapter four

In the Castle of Mote Ely

For the next half hour or so, Lily sat on the floor, shivering with cold. She wrapped her arms around her knees and buried her face in them, but without a fire or proper clothes it was impossible to get warm. A full moon shone in through the slit of a window, giving her just enough light to see by. There was a sort of bed, and a ragged old blanket on it, but they were very dirty and looked as if the last prisoner had just been dragged out of them. Lily didn't want to use them, in case they had fleas.

After a long while, soft footsteps sounded on

the winding staircase. Lily looked up. The door opened, and the small boy Gordon had called Rabbit came into the room.

He was carefully carrying a tray of food, and when he put it down on the floor, he gave Lily an anxious look as if he thought she might attack him. If she'd wanted to, he wouldn't have had much of a chance, for Rabbit was the wimpiest-looking boy Lily had ever seen in her life. Even if he had been standing up straight, he would barely have come up to her shoulder; instead, he seemed permanently hunched forward, as if he'd spent his entire life dodging blows. He looked about six or seven, but Lily decided from the expression in his pale eyes that he must be older than he seemed.

"Thank you, Rabbit," she said. Rabbit, who was pouring her some water out of a jug, jumped so hard he knocked over the cup.

"You remembered my name!"

"Of course," said Lily. "What's surprising about that?"

"Nobody ever pays me any attention," said Rabbit. "Except for Aunt Cassy. And Veronica and Murdo, of course, but that's just so they can tell me what to do."

"They seem quite good at that," said Lily dryly.

Rabbit took her remark at face value. "Oh, Veronica's really clever. I'd love to be one of her soldiers," he said fervently. "But she won't let me. She says I'd be an embarrassment."

"An embarrassment?" Lily looked at him curiously. "Why?"

"Because I'm her brother," Rabbit said, as if it should be obvious. "And Murdo's, too. Only I'm not allowed to mention it. Oh, dear. I suppose I shouldn't have told you." And he looked miserable at the realization of his own stupidity.

"Don't worry," said Lily kindly. "I won't tell anyone. It'll be our secret."

Rabbit nodded, then appeared to remember something. "Half-brother only. Veronica keeps reminding me of that. Especially when I make her angry."

The more she heard about Veronica, the less Lily liked the sound of her. "She's still your sister," she said. "She ought to look after you. Especially since you're so much smaller than everyone else."

"Oh, Veronica's not too bad," said Rabbit. "It's Murdo I'm really scared of..." But at this point, words failed him. For a moment his eyes blinked even faster than usual, and then, just like a scared bunny on the side of a road, he dodged away and disappeared through the door.

The guard outside spoke roughly, asking Rabbit what had taken him so long, and Lily heard him going back down the stairs. After a moment had passed, she bent and picked up her tray of food. The earthenware bowl of broth was fresh and hot and smelled surprisingly good. Lily sat down on the bed and ate it. She had just finished when there was another knock on the cell door.

"Come in," said Lily, and Gordon came into the room. He was carrying a black padded jacket and pair of trousers and had Lily's crocheted blanket over his arm.

"Here you are," he said gruffly. "I told Veronica she couldn't have it. She was pretty cross, but she knows I'm the boss." He tossed the blanket over to her. Lily caught it and wrapped it at once around her shoulders.

"The clothes are mine," he added. "They might be a bit big, but they should keep you warm. I'm still looking for a coat and some boots. I'm sorry. I didn't realize it was going to be summer where you were coming from. It's autumn here, and the foothills of the Black Mountains are always cold."

"Where are we?" Lily asked as she pulled on the jacket.

"The castle is called Mote Ely."

"Mote Ely!" Lily bit back the words that leapt inside her. Mote Ely was the place where Matilda Drakescourge's ghost had been sighted. But that was in Lily's own time. If what Queen Dragon had said about the Eye Stones was true, then she and Gordon could be any time in Mote Ely's past, present, or future.

"You've obviously heard of it," said Gordon. "Maybe you've even been here, in our own century. I'm not sure what the castle will be like, then. It's pretty crummy now, so I guess it will be a total ruin. We're now about two hundred years in the past, *our* past. The king of Ashby is Perceval the Peerless, and the Black Empire scarcely exists yet. But that's about to change. My ancestor, Raymond Longshanks, the original Black Count, is about to win the first of his great victories against the kingdoms at the foot of the

Black Mountains. In fact, I'm considering taking my army to help him. It would probably be good practice."

"Good practice?" echoed Lily. "For what?"

"For when I go back to our own time, of course. You don't imagine I intend to stay in this dump for the rest of my life, do you? I'm going to build my army up, slowly, and when it's trained and we're old enough, I shall go back to the Black Mountains and cast Sark out of *my* citadel. Then I shall reclaim my father's empire. All of it. Including Ashby." He paused, waiting for the effect of his words to sink in. "Unless, of course, you choose to accept the deal I'm about to offer you."

"I don't do deals with kidnappers," said Lily coldly.

Gordon colored. "That's not fair, Lily. From the moment I saw you in the well, I knew I had to do something. You and your dragon would have come looking for me; it would have wrecked everything I've been working for. You could at least listen to what I'm about to say."

"All right," said Lily. "Go on. I'm listening."

"I want your help, Lily. In return for Ashby.

Ashby should be part of the Black Empire. My father conquered it, and he was planning to reconquer it when he died. But if you persuade Queen Dragon to fight on my side, I'll let you have it. You can make yourself queen if you like, or give it back to those awful friends of yours, Lionel and Evangeline."

"I don't want to be queen of Ashby," said Lily in a firm voice. "I'm a Quench and duchess of Skansey, and that's quite enough for me. Besides, the kingdom belongs to Lionel."

"No, it doesn't," said Gordon. "But I won't argue about that now. What do you say, Lily? Will you help me?"

"I—I don't know." Lily did not know what to say. She could not tell Gordon what she really thought: that his offer was an impossible joke. King Lionel was the direct descendant of Perceval the Peerless, of Isabel the Magnificent. His own dead father, King Alwyn the Last, had fallen into a moat of flames defending his kingdom against invasion. She knew Lionel would rather die than be king of Ashby by the kind permission of the Black Empire.

"I'll think about it," she said cautiously. She

remembered the beads she had dropped on Merryweather Hill and wondered if anyone had found them yet. If she could only wait until morning, her friends might be able to find their way to where she was being held prisoner. "Let me sleep on it."

Gordon looked pleased. "That's fair enough. I'll speak to you again in the morning."

He banged on the door for the guard. Lily waited until he had gone, then pulled on the trousers and buttoned the jacket. They were soft and comfortable, and lined with downy padding that she knew would keep her warm. There was even a pair of woolly socks tucked into the jacket pocket. Perhaps, thought Lily, Gordon wasn't so bad after all.

She tucked the ends of her trousers into the tops of the socks. Then, after checking to make sure there were no fleas in it, she lay down on the horrible bed under the window, wrapped herself tightly in her crocheted blanket, and in less than a minute was fast asleep.

chapter five

Mystery on
Merryweather Hill

King Lionel woke up
surrounded by clouds of
smoke. *The house is on fire!* he
thought, and groped frantically
for Queen Evangeline. Then
he smelled a scent so distinctive
it was impossible for anyone
who had lived in Ashby Water
during the ten years of the
Black Count's rule to
mistake it. It was melted …

grommets, the same grommets that had poured in their thousands off the production line at the count's factory. A loud cough sounded somewhere close by, and Lionel realized that the smoke was pouring in through the window, and that Queen Dragon was standing outside.

"Oh, Your Majesty!" Queen Dragon hiccuped, and Lionel was almost blown out of bed by another waft of half-digested grommet. "Your Majesty, wake up! It's Lily! She's disappeared!"

"Disappeared? Queen Dragon, what do you mean?" Lionel started putting on his slippers. Beside him, Evangeline sat up in bed and rubbed her eyes. "Are you sure she hasn't just gone for a walk?"

"Come and see for yourselves," said Queen Dragon, and she left the window and started waddling at a furious pace across the garden. The king and queen pulled on their dressing gowns and followed her. When they reached the apple orchard, a terrible sight met their eyes. Lily's hammock had been wrenched from its bough. There were scuffed footmarks on the grass and every sign of a fierce struggle.

"But where have these people come from?"

asked Evangeline, bewildered. "Are there pirates or—or slavers around these islands?"

"Not that I'm aware of," said Queen Dragon. "There's only one beach a boat could land at anyway, and there are no footprints on the sand there. But I know that if Lily were still on the island, I would sense her presence. So I think it's a reasonable bet that she's been—"

"Kidnapped?" Evangeline's face turned white as she spoke the word. Then she spied something on the ground at her feet and picked it up. "Oh, dear. Look at this. It's a bead from the bracelet Lionel and I gave Lily for Christmas. I suppose there must have been a struggle, and it got broken."

Lionel looked at the bead. "Perhaps. But I'm not so sure. There's only one bead, you see. If Lily had broken her bracelet by accident, all the beads would be scattered here on the ground."

"What do you mean?" asked Queen Dragon.

"I think," said Lionel slowly, "that Lily may have dropped this bead herself. She might have left it as a sign for us, so we could tell in which direction she was being taken."

"You mean, like a trail marker?" said Evangeline.

"Yes. If I'm right, Lily's telling us to follow her. Look! There's another one." Lionel pointed, and Evangeline darted forward and picked up a small red object. This time, there could be no doubt. The bead was printed in gold paint with a single letter *L*.

"I don't like the look of this," said Queen Dragon. "Those beads seem to be leading somewhere, and I've a feeling I know where that is." She cast an anxious glance toward Merryweather Hill.

"Don't jump to conclusions," said Lionel. "Let's see if we can find another."

The next bead was on the edge of the orchard, and the next one after that was at the foot of Merryweather Hill. Lionel put it grimly into his pocket, and the three friends started to climb to the summit. The beads led, step by step, to the Eye Stone. The last one lay in the mud on the very edge of the brickwork.

"What a creepy-looking thing," said Evangeline with a shudder.

"It looks like whoever has taken Lily came through the Eye Stone," said Lionel. "The question is, where and when did they come from?"

"And where did they go back to," said Evangeline. She sniffed. "Do you smell something?"

"No," said Lionel.

Queen Dragon sat up on her haunches. "I do! It smells like... I don't know..."

"A swamp," exclaimed Evangeline. "It smells just like a swamp!"

"You're right, Evie." Lionel stood on the edge of the brickwork, peering in. Suddenly a terrible smell came pouring up the shaft, so strong it nearly knocked them off their feet.

"Lionel! Watch out!" screamed Evangeline, and Queen Dragon let out a roar of warning. But it was too late. Before their horrified eyes, the king dived into the hole and vanished.

"Get back!" Queen Dragon shouted. She brought her enormous tail down with a thump. Evangeline, who had been standing close behind Lionel when he disappeared, jumped back from the edge with a shriek. She lost her balance and almost fell down in a mud puddle.

"Sorry," said Queen Dragon. "I didn't mean to

give you a fright. But I didn't want you to jump in after him."

"It's all right, I'm not hurt," said Evangeline. "Oh, dear. Where's he gone? Why did he do it? Is he in the same place Lily is?"

"I don't know," said Queen Dragon. "I hope so. As for why he did it, I can't tell you for sure, but these things sometimes have a sort of pull that's hard to resist."

"What can we do?" asked Evangeline.

"I don't know." Queen Dragon looked worried. "Maybe I should take you straight back to Ashby. After all, if the king doesn't come back..."

At this, a look of horror came over Evangeline's face, and she burst into tears. Queen Dragon sniffed and smoked beside her.

"Oh, please don't cry!" she said. "I can't bear it when people cry. Oh, no! I think I'm going to cry, too!" A huge hot tear fell from her eye onto the edge of the brickwork, and then the two queens sat down together on the grass and howled. Evangeline bawled into her handkerchief, and Queen Dragon deluged the ground with bucket-sized tears of boiling water. Finally, when

Evangeline's handkerchief was so soggy it couldn't have taken another tear, and Queen Dragon had killed a large patch of grass, they stopped. While crying about the situation made them feel better for a little while, they were both too sensible to waste much time sobbing when they could be doing something practical.

"This is terrible," said Evangeline, wringing out her handkerchief. "If you're right, there's no guarantee Lily and Lionel are even in the same place. How are we ever going to get them back?"

"I don't know," said Queen Dragon. "Because I honestly don't know how to work this thing. You see, we dragons are magical creatures. When we see something like this, we know in our bones we should keep away from it."

"Couldn't it be turned into a good magic?" asked Evangeline hopefully. "If it was used for a good purpose, like rescuing Lily and Lionel?"

Queen Dragon shook her head. "I doubt it," she said. "People will never believe you when you say this, but there's actually very little good magic about. In order to get good magic, the kind that actually does make something out of nothing, instead of stealing it from somewhere or somebody else, the magician must be truly pure of heart. And there aren't many people like that around these days."

"That's depressing," said Evangeline.

"Yes, it is," said Queen Dragon. "But don't worry. I've a feeling that between us we might be able to do something."

"You mean, you've got a plan?"

"Not precisely," said Queen Dragon. "But I do have an idea. You see, the first time I saw Lily, I had the strangest feeling I'd seen her before. It was about two hundred years ago, in a castle somewhere near the foothills of the Black Mountains. It seemed so odd that I persuaded myself I must be mistaken. Now I'm not so sure."

"You mean," Evangeline caught her breath, "that it might really have been our Lily? That you met her back in the past, wherever it was the Eye Stone dumped her?"

"That's right." Queen Dragon nodded. "The only problem is, I don't know which castle it was. There were so many in that area at the time. It could have been any of them. But I do know I have something back at my volcano that will tell us where we ought to go."

"Well, what are we waiting for?" Evangeline jumped to her feet. "We must go and look for it straightaway!"

chapter six

Aunt Cassy

When Lily woke the next morning, she found to her surprise that a grubby coat and a pair of knee-high sheepskin boots had been put at the bottom of her bed. Gordon had kept his promise. The boots smelled awful, and the coat scratched her neck, but after a while she got used to the stink and the scratchiness wasn't so bad. By the time the cell door opened a short time later, Lily was starting to feel almost cheerful.

Her visitor was Rabbit, with a bowl of porridge and some black tea on a tray.

"Here's your breakfast," he said importantly. "Eat it up."

Lily didn't like being told what to do, but she ate the porridge anyway. It was sweetened with honey and didn't taste too bad. It would have been nicer with milk, but she supposed it was a bit much to expect that in the middle of a marsh. When she had finished, Rabbit put the crockery back on the tray.

"Come on," he said. "Aunt Cassy wants to meet you."

Lily was surprised. "I thought I was a prisoner."

Rabbit shook his head. "The general puts prisoners in the dungeons."

"Where I come from," said Lily, "anyone who's locked up is a prisoner, whether they're in a dungeon or not."

"You're not locked up now." Rabbit pointed to the open door. "Besides, you can't get out of the castle. There's no way across the marsh except by boat, and they're all kept under guard."

Lily rather thought this proved her point, but she didn't argue. She followed Rabbit downstairs and out into the castle bailey. In daylight, she could clearly see how badly the castle was crumbling away. Its stone bulk had been built on soggy marsh ground, and the foundations had not been strong enough or deep enough. Great cracks had opened up in the stonework and here and there sections of the battlements had collapsed completely. If it were not for the surrounding moat and marsh, Lily did not think it would be terribly difficult to escape from. She tried to remember where the watergate they had come in by the night before was, and wondered if she would be able to steal a boat.

A loud thud reverberated unexpectedly under her feet. It was followed by a grating noise and a hollow rumble, like a pile of rocks being dropped.

"What's that?"

"Oh, that's Murdo's gang," said Rabbit in an offhand voice. "They're just digging."

"Digging? What for?"

"Nothing in particular," Rabbit replied. "It's just something Murdo's been doing in his spare time."

He pushed open a door and led Lily into the dirtiest, mustiest kitchen she had ever seen in her life.

It was long and low, built into the walls of the castle and poorly lit by a glimmer of daylight from two barred windows. Turnip tops, potato peelings, old bread crusts and cheese rinds lay scattered over the central table and on the dusty floor. A tabby cat with a mangy, suspicious look about it sat chewing a bone in a corner; it peered at Lily and mewed a warning, as if it thought she would steal its breakfast. At the very end of the room, a clutter of dirty porridge pots and stew pans sat beside an enormous hearth. Lily's stomach lurched at the thought that her breakfast had been cooked in them. She could not believe that anything so tasty could have come out of such a disgusting mess.

Suddenly a pile of rags rose up by the fire. Lily nearly jumped out of her boots in fright.

"Oh!"

Rabbit hastily intervened. "Lily, this is Aunt Cassy. She does all our cooking and looks after us when we're ill. She wanted to meet you."

"How do you do?" Lily put out her hand,

though she didn't really want Aunt Cassy to touch it, she was so dirty and scary-looking. Her hair was gray and wild, and despite her rags there was something about her that reminded Lily of Queen Evangeline's mother, Crystal Bright. Lily was not sure what it was, but since Crystal was not a person she particularly trusted, it did not make her like Aunt Cassy any more, or change her first bad impressions.

Suddenly Lily realized Aunt Cassy was still holding her hand. She flipped it over and started looking intently at Lily's palm, running her fingers over the lines. Lily tried to pull it away, but Aunt Cassy gripped her fingers and would not let go.

"It's all right, Lily," said Rabbit. "Aunt Cassy knows magic. She reads palms and tea leaves, and even the stars. She can tell you everything about yourself, and your future, too."

Lily snatched her hand away. "No, thank you," she said sharply. "I'd rather find my future out for myself as it happens." As she spoke, a shiver ran down her neck and along her arm to the scaly patch of dragon skin on her elbow. The sensation was like lightning, so powerful it almost burned.

Lily had never before felt it so strongly, and as it subsided into frantic tingling, she knew without a shadow of a doubt that there was far more to Aunt Cassy than met the eye.

She stared Aunt Cassy in the face. The woman's gray eyes narrowed. Then she scowled fiercely at Lily and stalked out of the room.

"Oh, dear. Now you've offended her," said Rabbit in a worried voice. "That was silly, Lily. Aunt Cassy's a bad enemy. And besides, her predictions are really good. She's told me that one day I'll be a dragon slayer, and that when I grow up I'll be a hero and have lots of treasure, more than I can ever spend in my entire life. You ought to have let her look, you really ought."

Privately, Lily thought the chance of Rabbit ever becoming a hero was very small. But it seemed mean to say so. Instead she asked him who Aunt Cassy was, exactly. Rabbit explained that she had been the cook when the castle was first built, and that after the builders had left, she had stayed on alone.

"What happened to the others?" Lily asked.

"Oh, they had a plague or something," said Rabbit vaguely. "A lot of them died, and I guess the rest were all afraid to stay on. Aunt Cassy didn't have anywhere else to go. When we arrived, she was living by herself in the Marsh Tower. I think she was quite pleased when we turned up." The kitchen door banged open and he looked around with a start.

Veronica stormed up to them. "So this is where you're hiding, Rabbit," she said. "You're in breach of orders. Lily Quench was supposed to be locked up until the general called for her this morning. When I went to fetch her, the guard told me you'd already taken her away with you. And my pass key's missing, too. Where is it?" She held out her hand. After a moment's hesitation Rabbit brought a key out of his pocket and handed it over. Veronica dropped it into the pocket of her own coat and grabbed him by the ear so hard he yelped.

"Up to your old tricks, I see. I'll get Murdo to lock you up in the Backwash and see if you like it any better than last time."

Tears sprang to Rabbit's eyes. "Please, Veronica. Please don't. I'll do anything for you. It's terrible in there, and besides, tonight's high water, you know it is."

"As a matter of fact, I'd forgotten, but thanks for reminding me," said Veronica. "If you don't want to go in the Backwash, you should stop stealing and stop being such a horrible little piece of filth." She turned to Lily. "The general is waiting. He wants to talk to you."

"All right, I'm coming." Lily gave Rabbit what she hoped was a reassuring smile. She didn't know what the Backwash was, but it didn't sound very pleasant.

She followed Veronica out into the pale autumn sunshine. In the bailey, several squads of well-drilled boys and girls were doing exercises with sticks, marching up and down and shouting in a warlike manner. With a sinking feeling, Lily realized she was looking at Gordon's army. It was small, but still much bigger and better organized than anything she could have come up with. In a sheltered corner, a boy was lying on a blanket, ignored by the others and sobbing hysterically as if in terrible pain. Lily tried to look more closely at him as they passed, but Veronica marched her quickly by.

"What's the matter with that boy?" she asked.

"His arm is broken," said Veronica. "Tom's one

of Murdo's team. They had an accident in the cellar."

"Isn't somebody looking after him?" Lily asked, but apparently Veronica wasn't interested in answering her questions. She pushed open the door of Gordon's tower, and led her back up the stairs they had climbed last night. Gordon was talking angrily inside the throne room.

"Listen, Murdo," he was saying, "I know how keen you are to find this treasure. I know you're convinced you're getting close. But this is the third accident this month. All right, I know Tom wasn't killed. But the next one might be, and the troops know it. It's bad for morale, and it's got to stop."

Veronica knocked and pushed open the door. "Lily Quench to see you, General," she said, saluting. Gordon nodded and turned back to Murdo, who was standing with his arms folded grumpily across his chest.

"Dismissed, Murdo. And see it doesn't happen again."

Murdo and Veronica left the room together.

Gordon heaved a sigh. "I'm sorry about that, Lily. But Murdo gets careless sometimes, and I had to deal with him. Aunt Cassy has told him that a great treasure lies buried under this castle. He's been looking for it for ages, and he makes people do things that aren't safe."

"If it isn't safe, you should tell him to stop," said Lily. "What about the boy who was hurt? He ought to go to the hospital."

Gordon laughed. "Hospital? Lily, we're in the middle of a swamp. There are no hospitals in this time, anyway. Veronica will tell Aunt Cassy to give Tom a potion and splint his arm, and if he's lucky, the bone will heal straight." Lily started to protest, and he went on, "Listen. Things are different here. This is an army, and Murdo is a thug. When it's quiet, he gets bored, and then he can be difficult. It's better for me to let him spend his time down in the cellars digging for treasure, even if it means a few people get hurt along the way."

"I don't know why you don't send him away," said Lily stubbornly.

"Because I don't want to upset Veronica," answered Gordon. He changed the subject. "I hear Rabbit took you to meet Aunt Cassy."

"Well, he sort of did," said Lily. "But I'm afraid she got rather offended with me. I wouldn't let her read my palm."

"Stormed off, did she?" said Gordon. "Of course, she's quite mad. But she does have strange powers. For example, she knew immediately who I was. I was wandering about in the swamp after I came through the Eye Stone, and she went out in her boat and fetched me safely back to the castle. She said a raven told her a great prince was lost in the marsh, and she could see from my face I was the one. And she knows how to use the Eye Stones. That was how Veronica was able to bring you back here, to the exact time and place I wanted."

"Aunt Cassy can control the Eye?" asked Lily, shocked at the thought that Gordon might one day be able to bring his army straight to Ashby's borders. "How does she do that?"

"Oh, through magic and stuff," said Gordon casually. "She's got some potion she calls dragon's blood. It's a black juice that you smear or sprinkle around the Eye when you want to use it. It focuses the magic somehow, so you can tell the Eye exactly where to take you."

Lily shuddered. "It sounds perfectly evil and horrible."

"Don't be silly," said Gordon. "My father always

said there was no such thing as evil." But an expression crossed his face as if he were remembering something, and Lily knew he wasn't convinced by what he said.

"Queen Dragon says the Eye Stones were made by bad magic."

"Maybe." Gordon shrugged. "I don't really care, myself. Tell me, have you given my offer any thought?"

"A little." Lily's heart started to beat more rapidly. She hesitated. "How do I know you'll keep your promise?"

Gordon looked surprised. "Because I'm the Black Count, of course," he said.

Lily almost burst out laughing. Then she realized Gordon's expression was deadly serious. He wasn't joking. Suddenly it occurred to her that, whatever else they had been throughout history, the Black Counts had never been liars. When they said they would do something, like conquer a kingdom or burn a city or execute an enemy, they always kept their word.

"It's a funny thing, you know," Gordon continued. "Until my father died, becoming count was something I tried not to think about.

It scared me. I think that was Angela's influence. She was always weak and sentimental."

"Angela's not weak!" protested Lily. "She's one of the strongest people I know. And she worries about you terribly. Do you know she prays every day for you to come back?"

"Does she?" Gordon's expression was ominous. "Well, I hope her prayers aren't answered. I hate her. She loved that sap she's married to, Hartley, more than she loved me. Besides, it was her fault my father died. I'll never forgive her for that."

There was nothing Lily could say to this. Gordon had pushed his foster mother, Dr. Angela Hartley, off an icy precipice in the Black Mountains in a fit of blind rage, and the count had died saving her life. It had been an accident—the ice had cracked and collapsed under his weight—but if anyone was to blame for his father's death, it was Gordon. Lily was just thankful that Angela wasn't around to hear him talking like this.

Perhaps Gordon was also remembering what had happened on that terrible day, for his brooding expression darkened even further. "Well,

Lily. What do you think about my offer? Are you going to accept?"

Lily drew in a deep breath and summoned up all her courage.

"No, Gordon. I'm not."

chapter seven

Matilda Drakescourge

King Lionel sat alone on a tuft of marsh grass, trying to light a fire. Around him was nothing but swamp with forest in the background. He was cold and wet, and, since he and Evangeline hadn't had time to change before running out of the cottage, he was wearing only his pajamas, dressing gown, and slippers. Lionel had been through some bad experiences in his time, but at least he'd had proper clothes on. He thought he had never felt less like a king in all his life.

Not far away was the hole he had popped out of that morning. It looked a bit like a crater in the mud, and if he hadn't known it was really an Eye Stone, Lionel would never have given it a second glance. Of course, he'd tried jumping back into it, but he'd only made his feet wet and muddied the hems of his pajamas. The only thing that gave him hope was the small red bead he had found in the mud nearby, which meant that Lily was here, too. Lionel knew that if he went into the woods, he would lose his way. Cold and boring as it was, his best chance of rescue lay in waiting exactly where he was for Lily to show up.

"Someone's obviously turned the Eye Stone off," muttered Lionel. "Blast!" And for the hundredth time he wondered what on earth had induced him to jump into the Eye in the first place.

After a bit, Lionel heard something squelching through the mud toward him. He looked around hopefully and saw a large brown horse with an elderly lady on its back, followed by a smaller packhorse on a tether. The rider didn't look very dangerous, but Lionel had been through too many adventures not to know that you could never be sure. The newcomer might attack him out of fear; she might even be a robber. Lionel crouched down behind one of the stunted bushes nearby, and waited for her to approach.

Squelch, squelch, squelch. The horses picked their way across the dreary landscape. As they drew close, Lionel decided he had been sensible to hide. The rider was wearing a drab brown skirt and cloak and a hat with a red feather in it, but a large sword was slung over her back, and there was a bow and a quiver full of arrows on her saddlebow. Her hair was gray, her face wrinkled, and she had piercing blue eyes that reminded him of Lily's grandmother, Ursula, who had died not long before he'd become king. The packhorse was carrying a shield and armor. Whoever the rider was, she meant business.

Suddenly the afternoon sun came out from behind a cloud, and the woman's cloak shimmered dully in the light. With a loud cry, Lionel leapt out from behind his bush and grabbed the woman's bridle.

"Hey! That's Lily's fireproof cape. What have you done with her, kidnapper?" But before he knew it, Lionel's world turned upside down. "Aagh! Ouch! Eugh!" Lionel was lying flat on his back in the mud. The elderly lady drew her sword and jumped down off her horse.

"Kidnapper?" she said indignantly. "Who do you think you're talking to? How dare you frighten my horse? Who are you, and what are you doing out here in your dressing gown, anyway?"

Lionel scrambled to his feet and summoned up all his dignity. "I am Lionel, king of Ashby. That cape you are wearing belongs to a friend of mine who is missing. I demand an explanation of how you came by it."

"This cape was made for my late father, Sir Brian Quench, by the four-armed weavers of Skellig Lir, and bequeathed by him to me," retorted the lady. "And the king of Ashby is Perceval the Peerless, not Lionel the Pajama."

Quickly, Lionel put two and two together. "Brian Quench? You mean, Mad Brian Quench? Official Quencher of Isabel the Magnificent?"

"The very same," replied the lady. "And I'll thank you not to call him mad. My father was as sane as you or I—though sane people don't usually wander alone about swamps in their nightclothes. Who do you think you are, asking such impertinent questions?"

Lionel drew himself up. "As a matter of fact,

ma'am, although you may find it hard to believe, I *am* Lionel, king of Ashby—or rather, I will be." As he spoke, he extended his hand to show a ring on his little finger. It was one that had belonged to his father, and to all the kings and queens of Ashby before him. When she saw it, the lady went pale.

"Queen Isabel's signet!" she exclaimed. "I don't understand . . ."

"It is mine by right of inheritance," said Lionel, "just as Brian's cape is yours—in this time. I must apologize about that. In my time, it belongs to your five times great-grandaughter, Lily Quench, duchess of Skansey, who was kidnapped and whom I followed through the Eye Stone to this swamp. For your name, if I am not mistaken, is Matilda Quench the Drakescourge. Am I right?"

"Lily Quench," mused the lady. "Rotten name for a dragon slayer. Yes. I am Matilda Drakescourge. As for you, if you're the best they can do for a king in the future, then Ashby must be really down on its luck."

"I'm afraid it is, rather," said Lionel. "But we're working to change that. And this is what you can do to help."

In the gaslit treasure cavern under the volcano, Evangeline and Queen Dragon had just begun their search.

It was Evangeline's first visit to Queen Dragon's island home, and she was obliged to admit it was a remarkable sight. The cavern was filled with coins, jewelry, gold, and silver, as well as weapons and complete suits of armor. "My goodness, Queen Dragon," said Evangeline faintly as she looked at the glistening piles of treasure. "I had no idea you had all this."

"It's a bit of a mess, isn't it?" admitted Queen Dragon. "The rubbish heap is up the back. That's where I keep all the stuff that's not made of metal. We're looking for a yellow leather box, about the size of a suitcase. I took it from the castle I saw Lily at on an earlier visit, and I think the name was inside the lid."

Evangeline picked her way across the cavern. Diamonds crunched under her shoes and a ruby the size of a golf ball rattled away at the touch of her foot. As she started to sift through the jumble of clothes, gems, wood, and leather Queen

Dragon had not been able to eat, it occurred to her that there was enough wealth in this one cavern to rebuild Lionel's entire kingdom, pay for all the damage to Ashby Water caused by the Black Count's armies, and make her and Lionel the richest king and queen in all the world. But there was no point in saying anything. Queen Dragon had no idea of money or human values. As far as she was concerned, gold and silver were just metal, and to her, metal meant food. Besides, even if she did offer her help, Evangeline knew Lionel would be far too proud to accept it.

"Are you all right, Evangeline?" said Queen Dragon after a while. "You're awfully quiet."

Evangeline sighed and tossed a huge diamond over her shoulder. "Of course, Queen Dragon. I'm fine. Just tired."

"Make sure you rest if you need to." Queen Dragon looked worried. "Of course, I don't know much about humans, but when a dragon lays an egg, it's a very exhausting process. We only lay one every three or four hundred years, and it takes twenty years for the baby to hatch out."

"Goodness," said Evangeline. "How boring for you."

"Well, it has to be that way because we live so long," explained Queen Dragon. "Otherwise the world would be overrun with baby dragons. Not that I'm ever likely to have one. My fiancé disappeared through one of these Eye things nearly three thousand years ago. He never came back."

"That doesn't sound very promising," said Evangeline. "I hope we have more luck finding Lily and Lionel."

"Don't worry, I'm sure we will," Queen Dragon reassured her. "If we can just find that box, I'm sure it will jog my memory."

Evangeline picked up a pile of books with gem-encrusted bindings. They were ancient fairy tales, and she suppressed a pang at the thought of how much Lionel would love them for his library at Ashby Castle. "You haven't told me what happened yet, Queen Dragon," she said. "Lily must have made quite an impression for you to remember her after two hundred years."

"She did." Queen Dragon nodded. "I was raiding lots of castles in those days. The first Black Count, Raymond Longshanks, was overrunning all the little countries at the foothills of the Black

Mountains, and everyone was madly building castles to try and fight him off. Of course, for a dragon, castles are easy pickings. All you have to do is breathe a bit of fire, and they run inside and shut the doors. You can pick up cannon and all sorts of lovely metal without doing another thing. That's why I remember Lily. She was standing on the battlements yelling and waving her arms at me as if I were her greatest friend in all the world. As you can imagine, that was a bit of a surprise. When they see a dragon attack, most people run screaming in the opposite direction."

"I imagine they do," said Evangeline. "Hang on. I think I've found the box. Let's take it over to the light."

She stood up and carried the box over to the nearest flickering gaslight. It was broken and very dirty. Only a few shreds of the yellow leather remained on the outside, and inside the lid a hot iron had stamped the words **Crown Property: Mote Ely Ordnance**.

Evangeline stared at it. "Mote Ely. That's where Matilda Drakescourge's ghost was sighted."

"Yes." Queen Dragon looked stricken. "Oh dear. Oh dear, oh dear, oh dear."

Evangeline dropped the box in alarm. "Queen Dragon? What's the matter? Is everything all right?"

"Not really," said Queen Dragon in a shaky voice. "It's all coming back to me. Lily, I mean, and that dreadful woman. Oh, what a terrible day! I don't know what came over me, I really don't!"

"What do you mean, Queen Dragon? What did you do?" Evangeline drew a deep breath. "Queen Dragon. What happened to Lily?"

"She disappeared. In fact," Queen Dragon gulped, "I hope I'm wrong, but . . . I rather think I killed her."

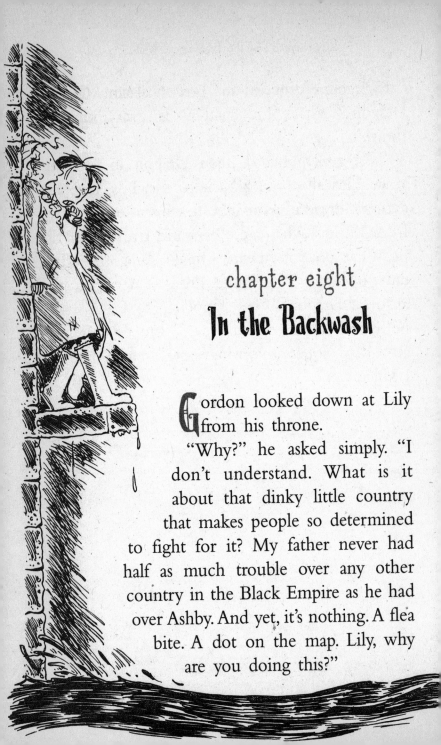

chapter eight

In the Backwash

Gordon looked down at Lily from his throne.

"Why?" he asked simply. "I don't understand. What is it about that dinky little country that makes people so determined to fight for it? My father never had half as much trouble over any other country in the Black Empire as he had over Ashby. And yet, it's nothing. A flea bite. A dot on the map. Lily, why are you doing this?"

"Because it's my home." It was the only answer Lily could give. She did not expect Gordon to understand, and from his furrowed brow, she could tell he didn't. But at least he didn't scream at her. The Gordon she had known in the past would simply have thrown an enormous temper tantrum, yelling and kicking and drumming his heels on the floor. He was still very angry—Lily could see that from the white edges to his nostrils and the set of his mouth—but he had learned how to control himself.

"I'd like to think you'd change your mind, but I know you won't," Gordon said at last. "You're no use to me, Lily. Since you know my plans, I can't send you back to your own time, but you can be an example to the rest of them here. Veronica!" As he called her name, Veronica came into the room. She looked slightly guilty, as if she'd been eavesdropping.

"Yes, General?"

"Take Lily Quench down to the Backwash. Make sure that Murdo's gang sees her put in there and that they're told she's been disobedient. When's high tide?"

"About ten o'clock tonight, I think," said

Veronica. She glanced at Lily, who stared at the floor, unwilling to meet her eyes.

Gordon nodded. "All right. That will be all."

Veronica called for a guard, and a girl with a striped shirt and cocked hat appeared at the door. As she left, Lily glanced over her shoulder at Gordon, but his throne was already empty. He obviously didn't think it worthwhile staying on to say good-bye.

Veronica and the guard escorted Lily into the bailey. Then they went into a small, square room next to the kitchen. It had a round wellshaft with a broken winch, and a rope ladder dangled down into what Lily supposed had once been the castle well. The guard in the striped shirt started climbing down the ladder into the shaft. Lily followed, her heart beating hard. Stumps of candles burned in crannies in the brickwork, dripping great stalactites of smelly yellow wax down the walls. As she descended she could hear the smashing, banging sounds of Murdo's treasure hunters getting gradually louder and closer.

About thirty rungs down, Lily passed the last candle. The ladder shook wildly below her, and she saw the guard swinging off into a dark, door-like cavity in the wall of the shaft. Lily reluctantly climbed the last few steps and jumped off into a vaulted cellar. Torches burned in brackets on the walls, and dozens of boys and girls were toiling away at the walls with hammers and picks.

Here and there sections of wall had collapsed and were being propped up with rickety wooden posts and piles of rubble. It was easy to see how the accident had happened. Lily thought it was amazing the treasure hunters' efforts hadn't brought down the whole castle. But perhaps they hadn't had a chance to do things carefully. Murdo was walking around the edges of the cellar, watching the workers closely and making sure no one slacked off. From time to time he shouted orders or abuse, or poked them hard in the ribs with a stick he carried under his arm. One girl dared to speak back. Murdo shoved her so hard she gave a cry and fell to the ground.

The girl's friends helped her up, and she returned, weeping, to her work. Lily was horrified. She wondered if Gordon knew what Murdo was up to, so soon after he had told him to be careful. Then she remembered that in the Black Mountains gangs of slaves had worked in the mines for Gordon's father, in conditions much worse than these. Gordon was just angry that Murdo had disobeyed his warning. Unless he learned to care about the treasure hunters themselves, there would never be any change in the way they were treated.

Veronica swung off the end of the ladder behind Lily and stepped into the cellar. "Murdo!" she called impatiently, "get over here, will you?"

A grumpy expression crossed Murdo's face, and he came over, smacking his stick against the side of his boot.

"What do you want?"

Veronica jabbed her thumb in Lily's direction. "Lily Quench is to go into the Backwash. Have you still got the key?"

"It's here." Murdo put his hand into one of his pockets and produced a key. "Shall I take her down now?"

"If you like," said Veronica carelessly. "The general says the treasure hunters are to watch. You might as well let Rabbit out while you're at it. He should have been in there long enough to pull him back into line." She turned on her heel and walked off.

"So you've been causing trouble, Lily Quench," said Murdo. He turned to the treasure hunters and clapped his hands loudly above his head. "Hey. You. Pay attention. This is Lily Quench. In the future where she comes from, I hear she's quite famous. So famous, in fact, she thinks she can break the rules. Well, she can't. Because at Mote Ely, if you don't do what you're told, what happens to you?"

The treasure hunters shuffled uncomfortably. "You get put in the Backwash," a small boy piped up at last. Murdo twirled the Backwash key on his finger.

"Exactly. Open the cover, Rosemary."

While the treasure hunters watched, Rosemary opened a trapdoor over a hole in the floor. A draft and a horrible scent came flooding upward. Murdo picked up a torch and prodded Lily in the back with his stick.

"Down you go. And remember: I'm right behind you."

Silently watched by the crowd of treasure hunters, Lily took the first step down into darkness. With every tread, the smell of damp and rot grew stronger, made worse in the enclosed space by the stink of burning pitch from Murdo's torch. He was following so closely that Lily could feel the heat of the flame on the back of her neck. At the bottom of the stairs was a door. It was made of oak and stained black with years of damp. Murdo unlocked it with his key and pulled it open.

"Are you still in there, Rabbit?"

A little voice came calling back from the darkness. "Yes, Murdo! I'm here!"

"Do you want to come out?"

"Oh yes, Murdo. Please. I'll be so good. I promise."

"Really?" Lily could tell Murdo was enjoying himself hugely. "Veronica thinks you've probably had enough time in the Backwash to teach you a lesson. I'm not so sure. Have you learned your lesson yet, Rabbit?"

"Oh yes, Murdo, I have. I have. Please let me out."

"Maybe later," said Murdo. Rabbit burst into hysterical tears, and Lily felt a hand shove her from behind. She stumbled forward, sloshing knee-deep in stinking water. Then the door slammed shut behind her, and she was in utter darkness.

"Is that you, Lily?" called Rabbit.

Lily stumbled forward. "Yes. Are you all right?"

"Yes," said Rabbit in what was, if anything, an even smaller voice. "If you walk toward me through the water, there's a sort of ledge on the back wall. I'm sitting on it."

"Keep talking so I know where you are," said Lily, but of course, this only made Rabbit more tongue-tied than ever. He gave a sort of gurgle and subsided into silence. Lily inched through the water. The floor was covered with horrible sludge and once or twice her foot nudged against some solid object that stirred and settled back again into the muck. Lily did not like to think what it might be.

At last her hand touched brickwork. Lily felt her way along the wall in the direction she thought Rabbit's voice had come from, and bumped into the ledge. A small soft hand reached down and fumbled for her in the darkness. With Rabbit's help, Lily hauled herself up onto the ledge. She took Rabbit's hand, and he gripped hers tightly in his own.

"Are you all right?"

"Yes," said Lily. "Are *you* all right?"

"Not really," said Rabbit, and Lily felt him shiver. "This is a terrible place. I have nightmares about it."

"You've been here before?"

"Yes. It's mostly Murdo who puts me in here. He's awful; he forgets he's done it. Veronica's usually the one who lets me out. But I must have made her really cross this morning. It was because I made her look bad in front of the general. Veronica has a lot of respect for the general."

"I can tell," said Lily. "Tell me, Rabbit. Why do Veronica and Murdo hate you so much?"

"Because of my father," said Rabbit. "He used to beat them. Then, when our mother died and they ran away from home, I sneaked after them. They didn't want me, but they couldn't send me back, because they didn't want me to tell my father where they were."

"So they've been taking it out on you ever since?" said Lily. There was no reply, but he squeezed her hand, and she guessed he must have nodded. "Rabbit, what exactly is this place? What's this high tide people have been talking about?"

"Well," said Rabbit, "twice a year, when there's

a full moon and the rains fall in the Black Mountains, the river that feeds the marsh has a flood tide. When that happens, they open the watergates so that it flushes out the moat around the castle. The water comes into this dungeon. I mean, really comes in, up to the ceiling. And when that happens, anyone who's in here... well..."

"Drowns," said Lily.

"Yes." Rabbit tried to sound optimistic. "If I'm lucky, Veronica might remember and let me out. She won't rescue you, though," he added hastily. "Not if the general's put you here. Veronica's very obedient to the general."

"Thanks a lot, Rabbit," said Lily dryly.

"You're welcome," said Rabbit in a puzzled voice. He paused. "Can I tell you something?"

"What?"

"Well," said Rabbit, "you must promise never to tell anyone. Not a living soul."

"All right," said Lily. "I promise. What is it?"

"Well... it's the treasure Murdo's looking for. It's on the other side of this wall."

"How do you know?"

"Because once, when Murdo put me in here,

he left me a light," explained Rabbit. "I explored the whole room. It's not very big, you know. There were skeletons on the floor, and people have written all over the walls—their names and stuff. In one of the corners, someone had knocked one of the bricks out of the wall. It wasn't a very big hole, but it was big enough to see through. And the treasure was on the other side." Rabbit sounded awed. "Lily, it's amazing. I've never seen so much gold and money and jewels... Aunt Cassy says a great hero hid it there, in a cave, hundreds of years ago. He stole it from the dragons who lived in the Black Mountains, and he washed in their blood so that nobody could ever defeat him. Then people came and built the castle over the top of the cave. Aunt Cassy says it's my treasure now, because I was the one who found it."

"Only if you can get it out of the Backwash," Lily pointed out. "It's no use to you, otherwise. Why don't you tell Murdo? If you did, he might treat you better."

"Because it's my treasure," said Rabbit stubbornly. "Aunt Cassy knows about it, but she doesn't care about gold and jewels, so it doesn't matter. And I can tell you because you're going to drown. But Murdo's not allowed to have it. He's scared of the Backwash. He never comes in when he puts me here, or he might have found it himself."

"I suppose so." Lily let go of Rabbit's hand and shifted her position so she was more comfortable on the ledge. When she and Rabbit had first started talking, the water had been below the level of her dangling feet; now it was touching her toes. For the hundredth time since her arrival at Mote Ely, Lily wondered whether Lionel and Evangeline had found the beads she had left for them, and whether they would be able to follow her through the Eye.

If they didn't soon, it would be too late.

chapter nine
Gordon's Dilemma

"So, what are you doing here, Matilda?" asked King Lionel. It was evening, and he and Matilda Drakescourge were sitting beside a campfire Matilda had lit on a bed of stones. Matilda was just dishing up a plate of savory stew made from a rabbit she had shot herself. It smelled delicious, and Lionel, who had eaten nothing all day, could hardly wait to bite into it.

Matilda handed Lionel his plate. "Well," she said, "I suppose you could say I'm on a quest. Have you heard of this pip-squeak Black Count, Raymond Longshanks?"

"I certainly have," said Lionel. "The Black Counts are a menace you're going to have to watch out for."

"Are they now?" said Matilda. "Thanks for the tip. I'll tell the king when I get back to Ashby Water. Anyway, King Perceval suggested I go to the Black Mountains and see if I can find out what the count is up to. There's been talk of a dragon in these parts, so this was the way I decided to come. But I'm not in a hurry, so if you like, I can take some time off to help you find this relative of mine, er, Rosebud—Pansy, er—"

"Lily," supplied Lionel.

"Lily. Stupid name for a Quench if you ask me. I called my own daughter Brunhilda, but she's turned out to be a real sap. All she's interested in is reading love poems. Must take after her father."

"Your husband was Lars the Horrific, wasn't he?" remembered Lionel.

"Horrific by name and horrific by dress sense. My father warned me, but I was distracted by the gold lamé and pink satin. Problem is, Lars is seventy now and still wearing the same clothes he did when he was eighteen." Matilda sighed.

"Oh well. We all make mistakes. And my son Rodney's not too bad, even if Brunhilda's a useless tub of lard."

Lionel finished his stew and put down the plate. "What do you think we should do about Lily?"

"I think we should go looking for her," said Matilda. "There's a castle not far away from here, across the marsh. If Lily's kidnappers brought her through the Eye, it's quite likely that's where they've taken her."

"A castle?" A thought suddenly occurred to Lionel. "Do you know what the castle is called?"

"I believe it's named after this marsh," said Matilda. "On my map, they call it Mote Ely."

In the Backwash, the water level had been gradually getting higher. It had reached the ledge quite a while ago, lapping around Lily's and Rabbit's feet, and then it slowly crept up until they were sitting in it and had to stand. Now it was creeping up Lily's legs. She had no idea how much time had passed since Murdo had locked her up, or when the floodgates would be opened to fill the Backwash completely.

Rabbit was starting to get anxious. "Veronica will be here to let me out soon," he said. "She's never left it this long before. Oh, I do hope she hasn't forgotten me!"

Lily didn't say anything. In the darkness with the water slowly engulfing her, it was hard not to be afraid herself.

Gordon sat in his private room and looked out of the narrow window at the setting sun. He felt depressed. Since he had come to Mote Ely, he often did, and he was sure there was something wrong with him. After all, his father had never been depressed in his life. Right now his father was the person Gordon most wanted to be like in all the world.

Lily was in the Backwash. Gordon had not wanted to put her there, but he had not been able to think of anything else to do with her. Now she was going to drown, and in his heart of hearts, Gordon knew that it was unfair and wrong. It was wrong because she was going to die and he did not want her to, and it was unfair because the real reason he was doing it was she had reminded him of his foster mother, Angela Hartley. Gordon did not like to think of Angela, but when Lily had told him how much she missed him, a picture of her had flashed into his head so strong she might almost have been in the room. She had been sitting in a chair, with her fair hair brushed neatly over her shoulders, and she had looked up, straight at Gordon, and smiled. Gordon had almost burst into tears. The memory only reminded him of how much he missed her, and how he wanted to forgive her, but couldn't.

Angela never said she didn't love you, a little voice inside him said. *She only said she loved her husband, too.*

But she promised she'd never leave me! Gordon raged silently. *She promised! She was going to leave me for him!*

But she didn't leave you, the voice reminded him. *When you went missing in Sark's revolt, Angela fetched your father and came looking for you. You never gave her a proper chance to explain.*

She killed my father.

Did she really?

Gordon buried his face in his hands.

A moment later there was a tap at the door. He looked up. "Yes?"

"The tide is coming in, General," said Veronica. "The boys down at the watergate want to know when they can flush out the moat."

"It's not high tide yet, is it?" Gordon felt slightly shocked at how quickly the hours had gone.

"No, General. But we don't have to wait until it's right up to open the gates. Can I give the order?"

Gordon thought of Lily in the Backwash and a wave of panic washed over him. She was going to drown. But if he gave the order to let her out, everyone would lose respect for him. A terrible pain throbbed in his temples, and he pressed his fingers against them. Veronica was standing silently in front of him, waiting for his order. Gordon opened his mouth, and then, like a flash of lightning, the solution came to him.

"No," he said. "Don't give the order. Not yet. I want to speak to Aunt Cassy first and see what she finds in my palm."

In the Backwash, Rabbit had become hysterical. The water had been slowly rising until it reached his and Lily's chests, even when they were standing on the ledge. They were cold, terrified, and disoriented. The suspense of not knowing what was happening was almost sending Rabbit mad.

"Veronica!" he cried. "Veronica! Please come and let me out! I don't want to drown! *Please!*"

Lily tried to reach for his hand, but he shoved her away. There was, she realized, no point in her trying to say anything. Rabbit was past helping. He would only push her off the ledge into the water, or worse.

There was nothing she could do, but wait.

The room had grown dark and Gordon had lit the lamp with an ember from the fire. Outside, cold marsh mists were gathering over the moat. Above the crackle of his fire, Gordon could hear the sentries walking the castle battlements and the lap of the rising water against its walls. A stray leaf blew in through the window, and he picked it up and put it absently into the fire.

Snatches of conversation came in to him from the corridor.

"Murdo. How can you have left him in there all this time?"

"I forgot."

"Forgot? You forget everything except your stupid treasure hunting. I told you to let him out ages ago."

Murdo growled something Gordon did not hear, and then Veronica said, "That doesn't mean you have to drown him. What would Mother have said? I don't care, you're going to have to let him out...."

Her voice faded as she and Murdo passed down the stairs together, and the room was silent again. Gordon put another log on the fire. For a moment, he thought he saw something flickering among the flames in its glowing heart, a shape like a dragon flying toward him. Then he felt a presence come silently into the room and stand behind him. He turned and saw Aunt Cassy. When he looked back to the fire, the dragon was gone.

"You wanted me, General?" Somehow, the way Aunt Cassy called him "General" made Gordon feel very small. She sat down on a chair. Gordon sat down, too.

"I want—" he began, and then, without asking, Aunt Cassy took his hand in hers and turned it over so she could see the palm.

"You want to know what to do about Lily Quench," she said.

"Yes." Gordon was startled, but only for a moment. Aunt Cassy bowed her head. Then she pulled the gray veil she was wearing over her face. Gordon was awed. The last time he had seen her do this was when she had told him he was destined to return to his own time and become a great ruler. When Aunt Cassy spoke from behind her veil, it always meant a very powerful prediction.

For five minutes or so, Aunt Cassy was silent. The fire crackled, the oil lamp flickered in the breeze from the window. Gordon started to grow stiff from sitting in the same position, but he dared not move in case he interrupted Aunt Cassy's trance and her prediction was lost. How much of what he had done since his arrival at

Mote Ely had been predicted by Aunt Cassy? Gordon could not remember now, but it was Aunt Cassy who had brought him to the castle, who had found lost children wandering in Ely Marsh for him to train as his troops, and who had told him what he must do to regain his father's empire. And she had given predictions to other people, too. She had told Rabbit he would become famous, and she had told Murdo that a treasure was hidden beneath the castle foundations. Everyone believed in her, even Veronica, who liked to pretend she was tough. And Aunt Cassy was the one who had stabilized the Eye so that they could travel whenever they wanted. The tiny dark smoky bottle of dragon's blood never left its chain around her neck; he could see it now, safely dangling there under the veil. Gordon wondered whether it was real dragon's blood, and then he remembered the dragon he had met in the Black Mountains, who had been Lily's friend, and suddenly his thoughts flew back to the Backwash, and still he did not know what he was going to do.

Aunt Cassy spoke in a low voice from behind the veil. "Know this. If you release Lily Quench from the Backwash, your plans will never succeed—"

Suddenly a bell started ringing in the castle bailey, drowning out Aunt Cassy's words. A girl screamed below Gordon's window, and there was a huge crash and a roar loud enough to split the castle to its foundations. Gordon jumped to his feet. As he did, a huge spurt of flame shot past his window.

"Attack! Attack!" shouted a voice below. "To arms! Soldiers, to arms! The castle is under attack!"

chapter ten

Attack of the Dragon

Aunt Cassy rose from her chair and pulled the veil back from her face. As she did, another shot of flame lit up the room as bright as day. Gordon ran to the window. A boy fell screaming from the battlements above him and splashed into the water like a stone.

Gordon grabbed his sword from its hook on the wall.

"It's a dragon!" he cried. "The castle is being attacked by a dragon!"

A strange, almost exultant look came over Aunt Cassy's face. Her hand went to the strange curved knife at her belt and she stood up, her gray eyes suddenly aflame with greed, desire, and a dozen other dark and dreadful emotions. Gordon ran out the door and down the stairs. The alarm bell was still ringing in the castle bailey, troops were running everywhere, yelling and screaming, and Veronica was standing on top of a staircase, shrieking orders no one was obeying. Her soldiers had been trained to expect a human invasion. Nobody had any idea what to do about a dragon.

Gordon ran to her. "What's happening?"

"I don't know. It just came at us out of nowhere. Nobody even saw it until it was right above us. Look out, it's frying the watchtower!" Veronica shrieked and ducked. A great fireball shot over their heads and hit the wooden watchtower on the ramparts. It burst into flames, and a dozen troops went rushing out its doors in all directions.

Half a dozen enormous cannon stood abandoned on the ramparts. The dragon picked one up in its scaly claw and shoved it into its mouth. The sound of its teeth crunching into the bare metal reminded Gordon of the night in the Black Mountains when he had met Lily's friend, Queen Dragon. She had introduced herself by eating his motorbike, and later he had seen her snap up fighting dragonet machines in midair. Ignoring Veronica's cries of warning, Gordon leaned out over the balcony and craned his head upward so he could see their attacker more clearly. It was a red dragon, with a familiar peony flush to its scaly underbelly, and it was so big it took up most of the ramparts along the north side of the castle. . . .

"Queen Dragon!" Gordon shouted. "Queen Dragon, is that you?"

The dragon ignored him. She was too busy eating, and anyway, there was no reason why she should pay him any attention. Gordon wasn't her friend. But there was somebody in the castle who was, somebody who could stop the attack with a single word.

With a curt order to Veronica to follow him,

Gordon ran downstairs and across to the well house.

The water in the Backwash was still creeping upward. It had reached Lily's shoulders a while ago, and was now gradually inching up her neck. Rabbit, who was much shorter than she was, was standing agonizingly on tiptoes. He had stopped crying long ago, but from time to time Lily heard him whimpering and splashing in the darkness. It was the only way she could tell he was still alive.

Suddenly, there was a creaking sound and a light burst into the chamber. Lily's darkened eyes clamped shut, and she cried out with pain. Beside her, Rabbit gave a great cry and fell with a splash into the water.

"Veronica!"

"Lily? Are you all right? Where are you?" Lily heard Gordon's voice calling out to her. Slowly, she opened her eyes and squinted toward the light. She could just see Gordon, with a lantern, stooping on the steps beyond the open door.

Almost fainting with relief, Lily cast herself into the water and started dog-paddling toward him.

Veronica was there, too. She and Gordon pulled Lily out of the water and threw a towel around her, and then Rabbit was behind her, somehow dragging himself out onto the steps. He dropped to the ground and wrapped his arms around Veronica's legs, weeping bitterly.

"Oh, for goodness' sake, Rabbit. Get up." Veronica pushed him away. "Blame Murdo, not me. I didn't realize he hadn't let you out."

Gordon turned to Lily. "We've got to get moving. Your friend, Queen Dragon, is attacking this castle."

"Queen Dragon? Here?" Lily's face lit up. Suddenly the bone-aching cold, the wetness of her clothes, the dreadfulness of her ordeal in the Backwash were forgotten, and she started stumbling up the stairs toward the cellar.

"Whoa!" cried Matilda Drakescourge. "Look at that dragon go! Where's my catapult, quick!"

Facedown in the marsh mud where he had dropped at the first sign of the attack, King Lionel found it hard to get quite as excited. The dragon had swept up on them from nowhere. Matilda's trained nose had sniffed a hint of molten metal on the night air, and then, like a thunderbolt, the dragon itself had shot across the moat above them, its fires burning everything in its path. Even Lionel, who had often ridden on Queen Dragon's back, was so stunned that he had been knocked off his feet. He scrambled to his feet, looked up at the creature on the castle ramparts, and grabbed Matilda's arm.

"No! You can't kill that dragon! It's my friend!"

"Your *friend*!" roared Matilda. "Man, what are you talking about? It's a dragon! Humans and dragons are natural enemies! We're like rabbits and dogs, or rats and cats! When you see a dragon coming, you kill it! Quick, hand me that saddlebag. There was a bottle of Quenching Drops in it this morning, if I can only—"

"No!" Lionel snatched up the bag, and they struggled over it. Then the king's foot sunk down in a muddy hollow, and he lost his balance. The bag containing the Quenching Drops was wrenched out of Matilda's grip and disappeared with a splash into the marsh.

"Aagh!" shouted Matilda. "Oh my hat! Those poor people in the castle! They're going to be fried alive! They're going to be robbed! What are we going to do?"

"Matilda, those poor people in the castle are our enemies!"

"True." Matilda remembered something. "But they kidnapped young Lily, didn't they? If she's in the castle, the dragon could kill her, too!"

"Calm down, Matilda," said Lionel. "You're forgetting something. Queen Dragon is Lily's best friend. The moment she sees her, the attack will stop. Look! I can see Lily now! There she is on the ramparts!"

And sure enough, as the full moon came out from behind a patch of cloud, a small figure emerged onto the castle battlements and ran toward the dragon, waving her arms.

On the ramparts of Mote Ely Castle, Queen Dragon paused in the midst of a delicious cannon, garnished with cannonballs, and sniffed the air. All around was the scent of her own smoke, but twining through it she could just sense the smell of a small, unaccompanied human. Queen Dragon blinked and peered through the haze. A short distance away, a girl with long hair and a beaming smile was running toward her.

Queen Dragon blinked. Her first thought was that this had to be a trap. This stranger must have been sent to distract her while her friends attacked from behind. Perhaps she was on a suicide mission. Queen Dragon had seen all sorts of things in her long life, and she knew that humans were apt to behave illogically in times of stress. She gulped down the last of the cannon, brought her tail down with a thump that shook the castle to its foundations, and prepared to defend herself against the enemy.

The girl was still approaching her, apparently fearless in the face of danger. Queen Dragon rattled her scales and drew herself up. Still the girl kept coming, and now Queen Dragon saw that she was waving, as if she were excited to see her. Alarmed, Queen Dragon opened her mouth. Drifts of oily smoke came pouring out, and she burped unexpectedly, sending a stink of melted cannon into the night. She wanted to shout, "Go away!," but instead a fireball shot out of her nostril in sheer fright.

Sparks flew, rock spewed upward, and the opposite battlements shook. For the first time, the girl faltered. She looked from the shattered ramparts into Queen Dragon's face, as if she did not understand, and then she started to speak.

"Get lost!" shouted Queen Dragon. "Leave me be!" She snorted again and blasted a hole in the ramparts at her feet. When the smoke cleared, the girl had vanished.

Queen Dragon was not sure, but she thought she had heard the girl shout her name.

chapter eleven

Rescue in the Marsh

Blown off her feet by the force of the explosion, Lily flew through the hole in the battlements and fell screaming through the air. A second later she hit the moat with a tremendous splash. Down she plunged, with all the breath knocked out of her, swallowing stinking marsh water as she went. In the darkness and confusion, she scarcely knew which way was up, but after a moment she managed to work things out, and kicked desperately for the surface.

A few seconds later she bobbed up in the middle of the moat, gasping for air. Queen

Dragon was still perched on the castle ramparts, breathing fire and chomping away on cannons. Lily felt dazed and devastated. Why had Queen Dragon attacked her? Surely she had come to Mote Ely to rescue her? Then the explanation came to her. Queen Dragon was over three thousand years old. The Queen Dragon she had just met on the ramparts did not know who Lily was and was not yet her friend. She had not followed Lily back into the past: she was already there.

Something splashed across the moat toward her. Treading water, Lily turned around and saw a coracle with an elderly lady in it wobbling through the water. Lily started paddling toward her. As soon as she reached the coracle, the lady put down her paddle and grabbed her. Hands that were unexpectedly strong heaved Lily upward, and she flopped into the coracle at the lady's feet.

"Don't wriggle so much!" said the lady sternly, and Lily crouched down on the floor and tried hard not to move. The coracle was made of skins stitched over a wicker frame, and she could feel the cold moat water slapping against her bottom and legs as they paddled away. After a couple of minutes, the coracle ran aground on what felt like mud. Lily's companion put down her paddle and hopped out. As Lily stood up, another figure waded out into the mud and water, and she recognized the friendly, worried face of King Lionel of Ashby, dressed in a grubby woolen dressing gown and flannelette pajamas.

"Lily! Thank goodness you're safe!" Lionel helped Lily out of the coracle and kissed her. Together they sloshed through mud and marsh water onto firmer ground.

"Did you find my beads? Did you follow me through the Eye?" asked Lily anxiously. "Is Queen Evangeline here, too?"

"Evie's still in our own time," said Lionel. "But we did find your beads, and yes, I did come through the Eye Stone. Lily, before we do anything else, I would like you to meet someone. This lady is your ancestor, the famous Matilda Quench the Drakescourge. Lady Matilda, may I present Duchess Lily Quench?"

The two Quenches shook hands.

"Pleased to meet you, my dear," said Matilda Drakescourge. "Pardon me for being personal, but you're awfully small. Are you sure you're really a Quench?"

"Quite sure," said Lily, and she pulled back the dripping sleeve of her jacket to reveal the patch of scaly dragon skin on her elbow. Then Matilda pulled back her own sleeve, and Lily saw that her whole arm was covered with curious glistening scales.

"Well, you've not got as many as me," remarked Matilda, "but you do have some, so I suppose I must allow you to be a Quench of sorts. The blood must have run a bit thin."

"My mother was a Cornstalk," explained Lily. "She was a gardener in the Ashby Botanic Gardens."

"A gardener? Dear me. The family has gone down in the world." Matilda started scrabbling around in her pack. "Here, Lily. Put on these dry clothes, and we'll have a talk about what to do next."

Lily stripped off her wet things and put on the clothes Matilda had found for her: a voluminous skirt and jumper, a petticoat, and an enormous pair of underpants. The underpants reached past her knees, but it was so good to be warm again she didn't care. When she was dressed, the three of them sat down on a rotted tree trunk, and Lily told Lionel and Matilda everything that had happened since her arrival at Mote Ely.

"I know exactly what Gordon's planning," she finished up. "He wants to bring his army back to his own time—our time—and take back his father's empire. And he can do it, too. There's this awful woman called Aunt Cassy, and she can make the Eye Stones take people wherever they want to go."

"Well, at least that explains why I ended up in the same place as you," said Lionel. "If we can find out how Aunt Cassy does it, it gives us a chance of getting back to our own time."

"Gordon said Aunt Cassy sprinkles dragon's blood around the Eye and tells it where to take her." Lily made a face. "I think it's real dragon's blood, too. There's something evil about her. My arm tingled like crazy when I met her."

"Hmm," said Matilda. "One way or another we're going to have to get into that castle. I've got some ropes and grappling hooks in my kit that should do the trick. Who knows? I might even get a shot at the dragon."

"Queen Dragon is our friend, Matilda, and you are not to shoot at her," said Lionel firmly. "Besides, if you kill her now, she won't be around in our time to help save Ashby from the Black Count. I'm sure you don't want that."

"I suppose not," admitted Matilda, though she didn't look very enthusiastic. "Wait here and I'll get my gear."

She trotted off, and Lionel took Lily's hand and squeezed it. Lily smiled as best she could. But inside, she was as worried as ever. All the talk of dragon's blood had set the scales on her elbow tingling again, and this time, it was not for herself, but for Queen Dragon.

Huddled in her flying coat and hat, with goggles on her eyes and a long scarf wrapped around her neck, Evangeline peered down impatiently from her perch on Queen Dragon's head. From time to time, through the cloud, she could glimpse the green patchwork that was Ashby, its fields and farms and woods. Any time now they would land in Ashby Water, where help was waiting.

"As soon as we've rested and had something to eat, we can leave for Mote Ely," Queen Dragon said. "And I think we should take Dr. Hartley with us, just in case there's been an accident."

"What are we going to do when we get there?" asked Evangeline. "After all, Lily and Lionel aren't at Mote Ely in the present. If you're right, they've gone back in time hundreds of years."

"I guess you could say I've got a hunch," explained Queen Dragon. "It's this story of Matilda Drakescourge's ghost being seen near the castle. You see, I'm pretty sure old Crater Face was hunting me in the woods near Mote Ely that time I saw Lily. And now she's been seen in the woods in our time. To me, that seems a bit much to be a coincidence."

Evangeline began to understand. "You think that Lily's right and there is no ghost? That the *real* Matilda might have found a way from the past into our own time?"

"That's right," replied Queen Dragon. "If Lily has gone back in time to Mote Ely, we know there has to be an Eye Stone there. And if Matilda's been coming through that Eye into our time, then maybe she knows how to work the thing. If we can make contact with her—"

"We might be able to get Lionel and Lily back!" exclaimed Evangeline. "Queen Dragon, that's brilliant!"

"Well, I thought it was quite clever of me," Queen Dragon said modestly. "As long as Matilda doesn't try to kill me on sight, that is. It's all coming back to me: something quite nasty happened that night. I don't know exactly what, though, because I was unconscious."

"Goodness," said Evangeline. She thought for a moment. "Still, you're here in the present, so we know you survived whatever happened."

"Not necessarily," said Queen Dragon. "When you mess around with time travel, the possibility always exists that you're going to change history. If that happens, and I die at Mote Ely, then Lily and I will never meet in the present to save Ashby from the Black Count."

"That would be dreadful."

"Especially for me," agreed Queen Dragon. "I really don't want to be dead if I can help it. Look, there's Ashby Castle! Hold on. We're going in to land."

Back in the past, on the shores of the moat, Matilda was preparing for the assault on Mote Ely Castle. She had tied a long rope to a special crossbow bolt and fired it across the moat into the castle wall. Then she had pulled the rope taut and secured it to the tree trunk they had been sitting on. Now, while Lily and Lionel watched, she pulled off her red leather boots and tucked up her skirts.

"How are you two at tightrope walking?" she asked.

Lionel and Lily exchanged glances. Lionel cleared his throat.

"Er, not very good, Matilda," he said. "What about you?"

"Oh, there's nothing to it when you know how," said Matilda cheerfully. "Well, if you can't rope walk, it looks like I'll have to go first and drag you over."

Matilda stepped up onto the rope. She tested the tension with her stockinged feet, took a hesitant step or two, then started running swiftly along the rope toward the castle.

"Wow!" Lily was impressed. "I wonder if she'd teach me to do that?"

"I can see it would be awfully useful," Lionel agreed.

Matilda's figure grew small and dark, and at length, with the moon behind the cloud, it was almost impossible to see her. Lily could not help feeling anxious. But Queen Dragon was still busy eating, and the occupants of the castle were too preoccupied to worry about human intruders. A minute or so later Lily heard a rattling noise and something came whizzing down the rope toward her. It was a pulley with a leather handgrip, attached to a long, thin rope.

"You go first, Lily," said Lionel.

Lily took hold of the handgrip and tugged the rope. Matilda started pulling. Lily ran a few paces forward with the pulley, splashing through the shallows, and then her feet lifted off the ground and she had to concentrate all her efforts on holding on.

Bit by bit, Lily jerked upward along the rope toward the castle. The rope creaked, and the pulley squealed under her weight. Lily's hands ached with the effort of clinging to the handgrip, and then they grew numb and she felt them start to slip. She saw the walls of the castle looming above her and Matilda's white face peering over the ramparts. Lily lifted her legs. With one last tremendous heave on the rope, Matilda pulled her over the stonework and dropped her safe on the ramparts.

"Phew!" Matilda whispered. "You're heavier than you look. Now for the king."

Although Lionel was skinny, he was much heavier than Lily, and pulling him up the rope took all of Lily and Matilda's combined strength. At last they saw his pajama-clad figure approaching the castle. Lily leaned over the edge to grab him and help him onto the ramparts. Matilda unhooked the pulley and spare rope and put them into a little backpack.

"We'll leave the main rope where it is," she whispered breathlessly. "We may need it to get away. Great fun, isn't it? I do wish you'd let me have a go at that dragon."

Lily decided it wasn't the time to argue. A flicker of movement caught her eye, and she motioned the others back into the shadow of a buttressed wall. They crouched down behind the brickwork, just as two cloaked figures came into view. Lily recognized them both at once. The larger one, leading the way, was Aunt Cassy. The other was Rabbit, carrying several metal buckets stacked inside one another.

"Hold this." Aunt Cassy stopped just in front of the buttress where the friends were hiding, and gave Rabbit a strange, curved knife out of her belt. He put it carefully into the topmost bucket. Meanwhile, Aunt Cassy lifted the cover on a pottery lamp she was carrying and poured something into it from a tiny bottle. A horrible, oily smoke started pouring out of the lamp. It sank at once to the ground and started creeping around their feet.

"Do I really have to wait here, Aunt Cassy?" asked Rabbit. "It's awfully dark and lonely."

"When I've killed the dragon, you can come," said Aunt Cassy. "As soon as I call you, bring the buckets. We'll need them to catch the creature's blood while it's dying. Until that moment, you'll just be in the way."

"I suppose so," said Rabbit forlornly. "Aunt Cassy, will I really be a hero after this? Will I really get the treasure?"

Aunt Cassy looked at him sternly. "Didn't I see it in your palm?"

Rabbit nodded, and Aunt Cassy lifted the little bottle she wore on the chain around her neck. Lily saw that it was almost empty. "With this dragon's blood, Rabbit, we will be able to go wherever and whenever we want. I've already told you I came to this time to find you and take you back to the past, where I come from. There, you are already a mighty warrior. The treasure of Mote Ely is your treasure, taken by right of conquest and hidden in the cave beneath this castle. If you do what I tell you this evening, I promise you that no one will ever be able to defeat you and that you will never be frightened again."

"Even of Murdo?" Rabbit asked.

"Even of Murdo," replied Aunt Cassy. "Now, wait here and mind you come when I call." She took the knife out of the bucket and paced off down the ramparts with her lantern, trailing smoke as she went.

"They're going to kill Queen Dragon!" Lily whispered. "What are we going to do?"

"I don't know." Lionel spoke softly, but not softly enough. Rabbit looked around sharply.

"Who—who's that?"

Lily put her finger to her lips and laid her hand on Lionel's arm. She stood up and stepped out from behind the buttress.

"It's all right, Rabbit. It's only me."

"Lily! You're safe!"

"Yes. Rabbit, what are you doing here?" Suddenly it occurred to Lily that Rabbit didn't look awfully pleased to see her. "Rabbit . . . surely you don't believe that rubbish Aunt Cassy told you?"

Rabbit gave a long wail. "You know about my treasure," he cried. "You were supposed to drown in the Backwash. Oh, my! What am I going to do? You know about my treasure, and you're going to steal it!"

"Rabbit, I don't care about the treasure. I promised you I wouldn't tell anyone—"

"I don't believe you!" Rabbit took a step away from her, then turned and yelled at the top of his voice. "Quick! Help! Invaders! Aunt Cassy! Come quickly! Aunt Cassy! *Aunt Cassy!*"

chapter twelve
Rabbit

Matilda jumped out from behind the buttress. She grabbed Rabbit, swung him up off his feet, and slapped her hand over his mouth. "You little rat," she said. Lily almost burst into tears. Their plan was falling apart before it had even begun.

"Now what do we do?" asked Lionel.

"We go after that old fright and stop her before she does something really dangerous," said Matilda. Suddenly there was a sharp struggle, and Rabbit twisted out of her grip. Matilda gave a cry of pain.

"Ow! The little brute bit me! I'm bleeding!"

"Rabbit! Rabbit, come back!" shouted Lily, but of course, it was useless. His buckets clanking, Rabbit had already run off.

"Let him go," said Matilda. "There's no point in trying to catch him. We'll have to think of something else."

"What's this treasure he was talking about?" asked Lionel.

"There's a stash hidden under this castle," said Lily. "Rabbit told me about it when we were in the Backwash. I'm starting to think it's all he really cares about." She turned to Matilda. "We've got to do something. Aunt Cassy's going to kill Queen Dragon so she can use her blood to control the Eye Stones."

"She's going to do more than that," said Matilda grimly. "Did you hear what she said about Rabbit becoming an invincible hero? The old dragon slayers used to try and bathe in the blood of a dragon. If they did, their skin could never be harmed by a dragon's fire, and they could never feel fear again."

Lily's eyes widened in horror. "Is it true?"

"Speaking as someone who's killed a good few

dragons and had plenty of spatterings, I've never cared to find out," said Matilda. "Dragon's blood burns. Besides, the legends also say that when you lose your fear, you lose your heart as well. Seems to me, my old father's fireproof cape is a much safer option."

"Come on," said Lionel. "We'd better get moving if we don't want to be too late to help Queen Dragon."

Queen Dragon had been slowly moving around the ramparts, eating up anything metal she happened to come across. She was now on the opposite side of the castle, her fires glowing contentedly. Lily could see she was getting full and was off her guard. She tried waving again, but Queen Dragon wasn't looking in the right direction. Instead, she was gazing dreamily at a tiny, gray-clad figure that was standing, surrounded by smoke, on the nearby ramparts of the Marsh Tower.

"Look! Aunt Cassy's putting Queen Dragon to sleep with that awful smoke!"

"Hmm," said Matilda. "An interesting technique. Rather unsporting, though. I prefer my dragons to be awake when I kill them. That lamp's nicely within range of the battlements. Let's get rid of it, shall we?"

Matilda took careful aim with her crossbow. But before she could release the bolt, a hand grabbed Lily from behind and flung her roughly against the battlements.

"Put down your weapons. And put your hands in the air," said Murdo.

Lily heard Matilda's crossbow clatter against the stone as she put it down. She could not see what was happening. Murdo was holding her, bent backward over the battlements; the blood was rushing to her head, and she could glimpse the stone pavement in the castle bailey far below. A waft of Aunt Cassy's evil smoke floated toward her. Lily knew that it was lulling Queen Dragon to sleep, and that the longer they delayed, the more danger her friend was in.

"One move from any of you and I push her over," said Murdo. "Now. Explain. What's all this about? Who are you two? And how did *she* get out of the Backwash?"

"I believe your friend the general let Lily out," said Lionel evenly. "He wanted her to stop Queen Dragon from attacking the castle. He knew they were friends in the future, and he thought she'd followed Lily through the Eye Stone."

"Murdo, listen," Lily gasped. "You have to stop this! Queen Dragon will be killed!"

"So?" said Murdo. "Why should I care?"

"Because..." Lily searched for a reason "...because of the treasure. That's why."

"The treasure?" Murdo's expression suddenly changed. "What do you know about the treasure?"

"Not a lot," said Lily. "But I do know Aunt Cassy knows more about it than she's letting on."

"Aunt Cassy's promised the treasure to Rabbit, as long as he helps her kill the dragon first," put in Lionel. "We heard her say so with our own ears, not five minutes ago."

"You're lying," said Murdo. "You can't have heard that. Rabbit's in the Backwash...." He looked from Lionel to Lily, and a note of fear came into his voice. "He's lying...isn't he?"

"Look on top of the Marsh Tower and see for yourself," said Matilda. Murdo followed her pointing finger. With a single bloodcurdling cry, he let go of Lily's throat and dashed off.

"Oh dear," said Lily in a shaky voice. "Murdo hates Rabbit. I hope he doesn't hurt him."

"If you ask me, Rabbit can take care of himself," said Matilda, picking up her crossbow. "Never make the mistake of underestimating someone just because they're small. Where's Murdo gone?"

"Not after Rabbit, at any rate," said Lionel. "He's heading down those stairs into the bailey. Come on, we're wasting time. If we don't hurry up, he'll be back with help before we know it."

The lantern smoke was still hanging about the top of the Marsh Tower. Aunt Cassy was sitting on the battlements, singing. She had a low, husky crooning sort of voice, and the song was gentle and rhythmic and strange to human ears. The poisonous smoke from the lantern went coiling and creeping down from the tower and onto the ramparts where Queen Dragon lay, half-sunk into a drugged slumber.

"We need to wake Queen Dragon up," Lily whispered. "If I go back around the ramparts the other way, I can sneak up on her from behind."

"We could certainly try that," agreed Matilda. "But I have to say, Lily, I don't like your chances. That dragon's drugged and pretty nearly unconscious. If she does wake up, she might attack you. Are you sure you want to do this?"

"Yes." In her heart, Lily knew the Queen Dragon on the ramparts was a stranger who had already tried to kill her. But there was no way she could stand back and let her be slaughtered in her sleep.

"All right," said Matilda, slipping off her fireproof cape. "But borrow this, just in case. Remember you're a Quench, Lily, and good luck."

Luckily Queen Dragon's attack had scared all the guards off the ramparts. Lily put on the cape and headed off at a jog. She soon reached the spot where Queen Dragon lay, snoring loudly and apparently fast asleep. Lily climbed onto her tail and started working her way up her steeply curving back. There was not much to hold on to, and the smoke made it difficult to see what was happening.

Suddenly, Queen Dragon gave a loud sigh and slumped down on her forelegs. The unexpected movement threw Lily off balance. She lost her footing and started sliding headfirst down Queen Dragon's flank.

"Help!" Lily thudded to a halt in the crease behind Queen Dragon's left foreleg, her head tangled up in Matilda's cape. She struggled to free herself. Again, Queen Dragon sighed. Then, so close by it made her blood freeze, she heard Rabbit's little voice pipe up,

"The dragon's asleep now, Aunt Cassy."

Lily wrenched the cape away from her eyes. Just below where she was sitting, Rabbit and Aunt Cassy were pulling themselves up onto Queen Dragon's front left claw. Aunt Cassy was still holding the horrible, smoking lantern, and the curved knife glistened in her belt. Together they started climbing up Queen Dragon's leg toward her shoulder.

Lily ducked quickly out of sight as they approached. Aunt Cassy and Rabbit passed her hiding place, and she crept out of the smoke and followed them all the way up to the flat bit on top of Queen Dragon's head. Aunt Cassy pulled the knife from her belt and gestured to Rabbit to hurry up with the buckets.

With a loud scream, half a war cry, half a warning, Lily ran forward the last few steps and flung herself into a dive.

"*Stop!*"

Lily cannoned into Rabbit's legs, and he fell over, dropping his buckets. At that exact moment, an arrow whizzed through the air from the ramparts and shattered the lantern in Aunt Cassy's hand.

"*Yah! Yah!*"

Brandishing her crossbow, Matilda swung herself up onto Queen Dragon's snout and started somersaulting toward them, yodeling a war cry as she went. Aunt Cassy made a dash for Queen Dragon's eye, but before she could reach it, Matilda was beside her. She seized her wrist and started wrestling for control of the knife. Rabbit pulled free from Lily's grip and started throwing buckets. One hit Matilda on the head with a loud clang, making her stagger momentarily. Aunt Cassy lunged forward and, with a cry of triumph, struck out for the soft bit at the corner of Queen Dragon's eye.

The knife blade dug in sharply. As Aunt Cassy wrenched it free, blood started pouring out like a fountain, trickling down over Queen Dragon's cheek and onto the ramparts. Lily cried out in horror. Queen Dragon groaned and started thrashing about in her sleep.

"Rabbit! Come quickly!" yelled Aunt Cassy.

Queen Dragon groaned again with pain, but the poisonous smoke had done its work too well, and she did not wake. Rabbit hastened over with his last buckets, eager to catch the pulsing crimson flow. Aunt Cassy prepared to strike again. Then a strange thing happened, something that Lily was never able to explain. Her arm tingled and shook, and a surge of Quench-like energy rattled through her body like an earthquake. The surge of energy flew between her and Matilda, and all at once Lily knew what Matilda was thinking and Matilda knew what Lily was going to do.

As one, the two Quenches ran toward Aunt Cassy. With a strength that was not just her own, but Matilda's as well, Lily ripped the knife from her enemy's hand and flung it away in a flashing arc. Matilda grabbed Aunt Cassy from behind and flipped her up onto her shoulder. With a mighty cry of triumph she spun Aunt Cassy around and hurled her, screaming furiously, into the castle moat.

"Matilda! Rabbit's escaping!" Lily dashed after him. Matilda unslung her crossbow and spun around, firing. Her bolt hit the bucket he was holding, and it flew up in the air.

Hot dragon's blood rained down on Lily's head. She screamed. It felt as if Queen Dragon's blood were eating through her skin and flesh and into her very bones. Because of Mad Brian's cape, only her hands and lower legs were exposed. But Rabbit was saturated. Blinded and squealing with pain and rage, he struggled with Lily a moment longer. Then his foot slipped in a blood puddle, and he skidded off Queen Dragon's snout into the great smoking pool on the castle ramparts.

Matilda came running over. "Lily! Are you all right?"

"I think so." Lily fought to collect herself, and felt the terrible pain already subsiding to a dull throb. "Matilda, what can we do? Queen Dragon's still bleeding!"

"Don't worry," said Matilda. "Believe me, it takes much more than this to kill a dragon. Give me the fireproof cape back, and I'll fix her up."

Lily untied the cape and let Matilda take charge. Her own hands and legs felt strange under their sticky, glistening coating, and the warm smell of Queen Dragon's blood went to her head, making her giddy. Matilda folded the cape into a thick square and pressed it tightly against the wound. Suddenly, Lily noticed Lionel was missing.

"Where's the king?" she asked.

"I made him wait on top of the Marsh Tower," replied Matilda. "When you're dealing with dragons, kings are a liability." She finished stanching Queen Dragon's wound. "Just as well my dry cleaners are used to me sending in clothes soaked in dragon's blood. I'd better keep the story of how I did this to myself, though, or I'll lose all my credibility."

"I'm sure no one will find out," began Lily, and then the sound of voices raised sharply below made her stop and look around. "That sounds like Rabbit."

"You're right," said Matilda. "And if I'm not mistaken, the other one is our missing friend, Murdo."

chapter thirteen

Gordon's Decision

Murdo had fetched Veronica from the bailey, and the brothers and sisters were fighting furiously, kicking and scratching and slapping one another's faces. King Lionel of Ashby was in the middle of the fray, trying helplessly to stop the three of them from killing one another.

"You've found the treasure! The treasure! Where is it, you little rat?" yelled Murdo.

"It's my treasure! My treasure!" shouted Rabbit. His face and pale hair were still coated in glistening dragon's blood, and there was something horrible about his appearance that went beyond even this. He was fighting so strongly Veronica and Murdo could barely hold him off.

"What's all this now?" Matilda and Lily jumped off the end of Queen Dragon's snout. Lily took hold of Veronica's arm, but the girl shoved her aside.

"You! You're the one who did this! It's your fault!" Rabbit jumped on top of Lily and started pummeling her with his fists. With difficulty, Matilda and Lionel dragged him off, and then Murdo jumped onto Rabbit's back and started hitting him on the head.

"Stop it! Please, stop it!" Lily cried. "Who cares about the stupid treasure, anyway?"

"I do!" shouted Rabbit. "It's my treasure!" With a swift, slippery jerk, he wriggled out of Murdo's grip and dodged away.

"Come back!" shouted Murdo. "Come back, you little toad!" He ran off, with Veronica hot on his heels, screaming abuse and threats as he went.

"My goodness," said Lionel, straightening his dressing gown. "This must be some treasure."

Lily was white-faced. "We've got to stop them!!"

"Hmm," said King Lionel. "Strictly speaking, Lily, this quarrel has nothing to do with us."

"But Rabbit could get hurt," pleaded Lily. "It was because of us that Murdo found out what he and Aunt Cassy were up to. If anything happens, it will be our fault."

Lionel nodded reluctantly. "All right. But don't take any silly risks, Lily. I want us both to get home safely."

The castle bailey was a deserted wreck. Most of Gordon's troops had run away, and the paving stones were scattered with huge sections of charred wood from the watchtower Queen Dragon had destroyed. Some chunks were still burning, and great sections of the castle wall had come crashing down. Lily knew there was only one place Rabbit would have gone. She and her friends ran to the well house. Sure enough, the terrible argument she had witnessed on the ramparts was continuing inside.

"Where's my treasure?"

"It's *my* treasure!"

"Mine!"

"Stop this!" A stern voice spoke over the others as Lily pushed open the well house door. "You are my troops, all of you," Gordon continued, "and I order you to stop this fighting immediately. I am the one who will decide how any treasure found in this castle gets shared out. If it belongs to anyone, it belongs to me."

"But I'm the one who's been digging for it," shouted Murdo. "I'm the one who's done all the work!"

"Aunt Cassy says it's mine!" howled Rabbit. "She says I'm a great warrior!"

"A great warrior? You?" jeered Murdo. "If you're a great warrior, how come I've been able to put you in the Backwash all those times?"

"Rabbit!" Veronica screamed, but it was too late. With a cry of fury Rabbit gave Murdo a huge shove. Gordon grabbed at him, Veronica caught at his sleeve, but there was not even time for Murdo to cry out. His foot skidded on the well stones, and his arms flew up. Then, cracking his head audibly on the stonework, he plunged into the well.

"I hope you die down there!" shouted Rabbit, and as he said the words he seemed to grow into something fiercer, taller, and more horrible. His face was red and blotched with anger, and his shadow loomed across the confined space. Lily recoiled, Lionel shrank back, and even Matilda jumped out of the doorway as he ran full tilt toward them and out into the night. For a moment, they heard his footsteps ringing out in the castle bailey. Then they faded into silence and he was gone.

"Rabbit! Murdo! Rabbit!" Veronica was screaming hysterically, pulling her hair and stuffing her fingers into her mouth. Lily went over and tried to put her arms around her, but she fought against her embrace. Gordon leaned over the rim of the well. His voice echoed horribly in the narrow space as he shouted down the shaft.

"Murdo! *Murdo!*"

There was no reply.

"Do you think he could have survived?" asked Lionel.

At this, Veronica gave a great howl and sat down with a thump on the well house floor. She buried her face in her knees and sobbed uncontrollably. Once more, Lily tried to comfort her, but it was impossible to calm her down.

"Leave her be, Lily," said Gordon quietly. "I

know exactly how she feels. There's absolutely nothing you can do to make her feel any better." He paused, and Lily knew he was remembering his father and that dreadful day above Dragon's Downfall in the Black Mountains. "All we can do is send someone down to look."

"I'll go," said Lily at once.

"No," said Gordon. "Or at least, not on your own, Lily. They're my troops. If you're going down that well, I'm coming, too."

Gordon fetched a lantern he had brought with him into the well house. He turned up the wick and hooked it onto his belt, then swung his legs into the well. Lily followed him down the ladder. Some of the treasure hunters' candles were still burning in their sconces on the walls, but after they climbed past the opening to the cellar, there was only Gordon's lantern to show the way. Fortunately, the shaft was not as deep as it looked from the top. There was no water at the bottom, and when Lily jumped off the end of the ladder, she landed knee-deep in slush and rubbish.

Murdo was lying nearby, faceup in the mud, with his eyes closed. Blood streaked his face and hair, and he was deathly pale but still breathing.

Then Gordon shone his light over his unconscious body. Lily winced and gasped. Both Murdo's legs were twisted at horrible angles, broken.

"Look at his legs," said Gordon in a low voice. "In this place and time, even one broken bone might kill him, but with really bad injuries like these..." Suddenly his voice caught. "Oh, Lily. What am I going to tell Veronica?"

"There is one possibility," said Lily. "You might not like it, but... if we can take Murdo back to our own time, Angela might be able to help him. She can set his broken bones and treat his injuries—" Lily hesitated. "I don't know. He might still die. He might die before we can even get him back there. But at least in our time, he can go to the hospital. At least Angela can give him a chance of pulling through."

Gordon sat thinking. The lantern light flickered over his features, and Lily thought his face was drawn and sadder than anything she had ever seen in her life. Yet she knew Gordon's memories of his father's death were nothing to whether he really believed the lie he had told himself. If Gordon truly believed in his heart that Angela had killed his father, that she had abandoned him, and that she didn't love him, then Lily knew he would be cruel enough to put Veronica through the same piercing sadness he had known himself.

A change came over his expression, and Lily saw that in that moment, he had come to a decision.

"All right," said Gordon. "I agree."

Hoisting Murdo out of the shaft was a painful, dangerous business. It took them quite a while to decide how to do it. In the end Matilda splinted his legs, and they hauled him up, strapped to an old plank of wood, while Gordon steadied his passage from below with a guide rope. Once or twice their makeshift stretcher banged against the wall of the well shaft, but Murdo was so deeply unconscious he never stirred or opened his eyes. By the time they got him out into the castle bailey his color was even more dreadful than it had appeared in the well, and his breathing was painful to listen to.

Veronica sat by the stretcher, crying and holding her brother's hand.

"I always knew Rabbit would do something terrible one day," she sobbed. "He was always telling lies. He used to do awful things, and then tell his father it was me or Murdo."

"That wasn't enough of a reason for Murdo to put Rabbit in the Backwash," pointed out Lily gently.

"No," said Veronica. "But Murdo never forgave him for the way his father treated our mother, and there was a lot of his father in Rabbit. And now he's gone, and Murdo is going to die, and I'm going to be all on my own." And she broke down in a new storm of weeping.

"We don't know for sure that Murdo is going to die," said Lily. "If he gets better, I know he'll come back from the future and find you. And besides, you'll still have Gordon. I know he thinks an awful lot of you."

"Does he really?" Veronica seemed quite impressed.

Lily nodded. "He thinks you're really clever. He'd like you for a friend. Now his army's gone, he's going to need you more than ever."

Just then, Gordon himself appeared with Matilda and Lionel. "Everything's ready," he said.

"We've organized some boats to take you across the moat to the Eye Stone. By the way, I've decided to send Tom with you, too. We found him on his own in the barracks; everyone else had run off. I figured Angela could set his arm while she was at it."

Lily smiled. "I think that's an excellent idea."

"You'll have to be careful," said Gordon. "Rabbit and Aunt Cassy are out there in the marsh somewhere. Rabbit seems determined to get that treasure, and after what they did this evening, I don't trust them a bit."

"I wouldn't worry too much," said Matilda. "I think you'll find they've gone back in time through the Eye. As for the treasure, if you can find it, it's yours. But I don't like your chances. I passed your relative, Raymond Longshanks, camped out in the marsh with his army, about twenty miles back. He's marching toward this castle. I imagine he'll arrive some time tomorrow."

"Raymond is coming here?" Gordon's face lit up. "That's tremendous news! Lily, Lionel"—he turned to the king—"I give you fair notice. I *will* come back to our own time, and I *will* claim my father's empire. But I will make a deal with you. When I come, I will send Ashby a warning first. My father always gave his enemies a chance to surrender before he attacked them, and like him, I am a man of my word."

"Thank you," said Lionel gravely. He and Gordon shook hands, and Lily put her own hand on theirs to seal the bargain.

For a moment they stood in silent agreement. Then there was a commotion on the battlements: a sound of scaly wings swooping in and out, and a dragonish cry. A whoosh of warm air swept down from the ramparts over their upturned faces, and there came the beating of giant wings overhead.

Queen Dragon had woken up and flown away.

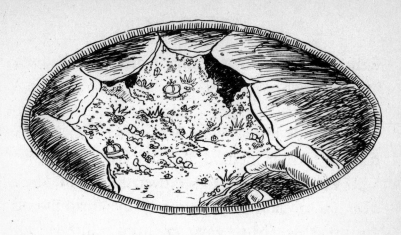

chapter fourteen

The Claiming of the Treasure

The birds were singing, and it was a fine summer afternoon. Queen Dragon, Dr. Angela Hartley, and Queen Evangeline of Ashby were sitting in the sunshine in the woods of Mote Ely. Queen Dragon, whose appetite was rarely troubled by danger or misfortune, was eating an old car wreck. The two humans were trying to interest themselves in a picnic of ham sandwiches, bananas, and fruit cake from the Ashby Castle kitchens, but neither of them was having much success.

A loud shriek pierced the air not far away.

Evangeline started, and Angela nearly choked on her sandwich.

"What was that?"

"It sounds like somebody's been hurt." Angela reached for her medical bag, and Queen Dragon, who was tall enough to see over the surrounding trees, sat up and peered around the surrounding countryside. She gave a loud squawk of excitement, and a car door dropped with a crash from her mouth onto the ground.

"It's Lily and Lionel! And—and some other people! They're coming toward us!"

A loud whistle sounded through the trees in front of them, and then there was a rustle of bushes and a strange lady in a brown skirt and jaunty hat appeared. She was followed by a boy with his arm in a sling, and Lily and Lionel carrying a stretcher. Angela took one look at Lily's blood-soaked clothes and rushed toward her. Lily and the king of Ashby set down the stretcher, and Lionel flung himself into Queen Evangeline's arms.

"It's all right, Angela, I'm not hurt," said Lily reassuringly. "But Murdo and Tom here need your help at once. Poor Murdo got a bit bumped when we brought him through the Eye." And indeed, Murdo was moaning on his stretcher and looking in a very bad way indeed.

Queen Dragon sniffed Lily's skirt suspiciously. "If I'm not mistaken, that's dragon's blood." She looked from Lily to Matilda Drakescourge and bared her teeth. "You. It was you, wasn't it? Have you been killing any more of my relatives, Crater Face?"

"I most certainly have not!" retorted Matilda. "As a matter of fact, I've been saving your life, you ungrateful creature, so before you call me Crater Face again, I'd ask you to think twice and remember I've got a bottle of Quenching Drops in my pocket!"

"It's all right, Queen Dragon!" said Lily hastily. "Matilda isn't an enemy this time. She's a friend."

"Some friend!" hissed Queen Dragon, and she lashed her tail so hard it brought down an enormous tree that was just behind her. Fortunately at this point, Angela interrupted the conversation.

"You're right, Lily. Murdo here needs to get to the hospital as soon as he can," she said. "I can strap his legs and clean him up a bit, and give him an injection for the pain, but he's a very sick boy. Queen Dragon, can you fly us back to Ashby Water as soon as possible?"

Queen Dragon simmered down a little. "Of course, Angela. We'll leave right away."

"Come back quickly when you're finished, Queen Dragon," said Lionel. "And send some armored trucks and guards by road. I've a feeling we might be needing them."

Wrapped up warmly and strapped to makeshift stretchers, Murdo and Tom were hoisted onto Queen Dragon's head and tied in place. Angela hopped up beside them. She waved to everyone on the ground, and then the dragon ambulance sprang into the air and veered off in the direction of Ashby Water.

Lily waved good-bye with mixed feelings. She was not altogether certain she wanted Murdo in Ashby Water. He had not been very nice to her, and she knew she would remember her ordeal in the Backwash until the day she died. Then she remembered what Mr. Hartley said: that the worse someone was, the better it was for them and everybody else when they turned around and started afresh. The thought cheered her up a little, and while they were waiting for Queen Dragon to come back, she went off with Matilda and the king and queen to have a look at the castle.

Gordon's guess had been right: in their own time, Mote Ely Castle was nothing but a ruin. It looked sad and forgotten. The Marsh Tower had completely collapsed, the walls were crumbling, and there was nothing left of the moat but a grassy depression. Around and about, Ely Marsh was being drained and gradually turned into farmland. Even the woods were disappearing. Lily could see patches where whole copses had been felled, and she could hear the sound of woodcutters working among the trees.

Together, Lily and her friends walked across the old moat to the main entrance of the castle. The mighty iron-clad gate had long since disappeared and the castle bailey was overgrown with weeds. It was all so changed that at first it was hard for Lily to work out where she was, but after a while she recognized some windows and was able to get her bearings. The well house was completely gone. Its roof and walls had fallen in, but when they went into the kitchen, they found that its stone floor had collapsed into the old cellars where Murdo's treasure hunters had done their digging. With Matilda's ropes, it was an easy matter to let themselves down into the space below.

"Will you be all right, Evie?" Lionel asked.

"Of course," said Evangeline. "I'm not that fat, you know. Besides, I wouldn't miss out on this for anything."

The kitchen roof had been taken away long ago by local scavengers, and a filtered sunlight shone over the cellar floor. Lily found the entrance to the Backwash quickly. The trapdoor had rotted away, and it was easy to smash through the last few bits of wood. Evangeline handed around some torches she had brought from Ashby, and they turned them on and went down the steps into the dungeon where Lily had almost drowned two hundred years before.

Because the moat was empty, the Backwash was no longer filled with water. Its floor was covered with ancient, dried-up mud and rubbish, and there was a jumble of bones, both animal and human, in one of the corners. A few cockroaches ran away from their torches as they shone them over the walls, which were covered with carvings:

prayers and curses, names and dates, the hopes and fears and despair of all the prisoners who had ever died here. Tucked away in a corner, Lily could just make out a single word, *rabit*, scratched on the stone. A lump came into her throat, and she turned away.

"I promised him I would never tell a living soul where his treasure was," she said. "But all the people who were alive then are dead in our time, so I guess it doesn't matter anymore. Rabbit said there was a hole in the corner, up near the ceiling. The treasure was in a cave on the other side."

"There's a sort of crack over there," said Evangeline, pointing. "Do you think that could be what he was talking about?"

"Perhaps." Lionel climbed up onto a broken ledge of bricks and inched along until he reached the crack. He poked his long fingers into it and flicked out some dried mud and dirt. He shone his torch into the hole and was silent for a long time.

At last Evangeline cleared her throat. "Can you see anything?"

"Yes," said Lionel. "I can. It's amazing."

The king turned around, and Lily saw that he was crying. Then Matilda produced a hammer and the wall was breached and the names of all the prisoners lay crumbled and shattered in the dust. And in the cave beyond the wall were wonderful things, a treasure richer and more beautiful than anything Lily could have imagined, a treasure that made her and Lionel and Evangeline dance and weep with joy. For what was there was enough to make Ashby the richest kingdom east of the Black Mountains. After long years of poverty and hardship, Ashby Water and its castle could be rebuilt. All the citizens would have jobs and enough to eat, and Ashby could grow strong and defend itself against General Sark, or Gordon, or any other enemy who came against it.

And when Queen Dragon returned at nightfall, with the news that Tom and Murdo were safe in the hospital and as well as could be expected, and that some trucks and guards were leaving Ashby Water that very evening, a huge party was held in the castle bailey, with sandwiches and fruitcake and a whole roast lamb killed by Matilda and cooked by Queen Dragon. Everybody dined off silver plates and toasted one another with sapphire-studded goblets, and Queen Dragon nobly refrained from eating the dishes. Then Matilda got excited and kissed her, and Queen Dragon took her for a spin through the clouds, laughing and whooping and shooting triumphant fireballs into the dark. And that night it was a long time before anyone went to sleep, or stopped talking about their wonderful discovery.

After that, only one thing remained to be done.

"Matilda," said Lionel the following morning as they stood beside the Eye Stone, "we'd like to thank you. Without your help, this adventure could never have ended as happily as it has. I wish there was something we could do to reward you, but I don't think any grants or honors I could offer would count in your own time."

"Oh, never mind," said Matilda good-naturedly. "It'll be a tremendous story to tell King Perceval when I see him; that's all I care about."

"There's one more thing we need you to do before you go back to him, however," said Lionel. "You see, Matilda, we've been playing around with time, and that makes all sorts of funny things happen. When Lily and I went back into the past, we created a big loop with the present. What we did in your day affects not only what happened then, but also what has happened, and is going to happen here in our time."

"It's important to make sure that none of us does anything to break that time loop, otherwise history will be changed," explained Evangeline. "This whole adventure was set off by you, Matilda. A few weeks ago, some woodcutters claimed to have seen your ghost in the woods near this castle. What we think they really saw was you, popping out of the Eye Stone. Would you mind going through the Eye to those dates and pretending to be a ghost? Because if you don't appear on those dates, the events of the last few weeks will be changed. Lionel and I will never ask Lily to investigate the mystery, and the Treasure of Mote Ely will never be found."

"I'm not sure I like the thought of impersonating my own ghost," mused Matilda. "But I suppose Ashby does need the treasure. All right. When's this ghost supposed to have been seen?"

Evangeline produced a newspaper from her knapsack. "The first appearance was three weeks ago."

"Right-oh."

While Matilda waited, Queen Dragon dug a claw into one of her own scaly feet. "Ouch," she said. "That hurt. Still, I suppose it's nothing compared to what that Cassy creature wanted to do to me." She carefully let a single blood drop fall on the opening to the Eye, and Matilda jumped in, shouting out the date. A few minutes went by and she popped back out of the hole like a rabbit out of a magician's hat.

"Done," she said. "Saw a couple of woodcutters in the forest having a picnic lunch, so I jumped out and went *Boo!* I made one faint and the other drop his sandwich in a mud puddle. What's next?"

Evangeline read quickly through the list of dates when the "ghost" had appeared, and one by one, Matilda visited them through the Eye. When she had finished, and it was time for her to go, there were tears in everybody's eyes.

"Come on, Lily. Give us a kiss," said Matilda, and Lily went over and put her arms around her.

It was uncannily like hugging her grandmother Ursula, except that somehow Matilda was not as big as Ursula had been. Or maybe Lily herself was bigger, for it was now almost a year and many adventures since her grandmother had died. Everything had changed so much it was sometimes hard for her to believe she was the same person. But it had mostly changed for the better, and Lily hoped in her heart that the best times were yet to come.

"Back to my own time now," said Matilda. "See you later, dragon. I look forward to our next fight." And with a jaunty wave, she shouted the date and stepped into the hole, disappearing into the past forever.

"Hmm," said Queen Dragon. "I don't like the sound of that."

"Don't worry, Queen Dragon," said Evangeline. "Think of it this way. Any fight Matilda's going to have with you in the past has already happened to you."

"That's true," said Queen Dragon, brightening up. "And the blood on the Eye Stone is dry now, so she can't come back. Especially if we can find a way of closing it off permanently."

Soon after this, the trucks and guards arrived from Ashby Water, along with a car for the king and queen, and the Treasure of Mote Ely was loaded into strongboxes. Queen Dragon and Lily stood on the ruined ramparts of Mote Ely Castle and watched the motorcade drive off.

"You know, it's funny what people think of as treasure," said Queen Dragon to Lily. "I've got a whole cave of this stuff back at the volcano. You humans get so excited about something I just think of as dinner. If you'd only asked, I'd have given you whatever you wanted."

"Would you really?" asked Lily.

"Of course I would. Wouldn't you share your dinner with a friend?"

"I'd never thought of it like that," said Lily.

"Maybe that's why humans and dragons have had so many arguments over the years," said Queen Dragon. "It would be nice if things could change."

"They already have," said Lily, and she looked at her hands, resting on the castle walls, and smiled. Where Queen Dragon's blood had drenched her skin, a new soft covering of tiny dragon scales was already forming, like the ones on her elbow. As for her heart, well, it certainly felt like it was still there, but a new courage was in it, a courage that would take her on to further adventures and greater feats. Lily did not know yet what those might be. But she did know that wherever she went, and whatever adventures she had, Queen Dragon would be with her.

Impulsively, she leaned her cheek against Queen Dragon's scaly leg and kissed her.

"Things have already changed, Queen Dragon," she said. "They already have."

Don't miss these other
exciting adventures. . . .

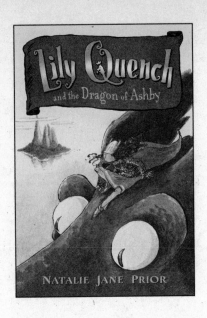

Lily Quench and the Dragon of Ashby

As a family of dragon slayers, the Quenches of Ashby have always been burning successes... until the evil Black Count invades, and the family's fortunes go into a downward spiral.

Then a dragon unexpectedly arrives and Lily, the last of the Quenches, is called upon to fight it. Soon she finds herself on a desperate, magical quest to save Ashby from destruction—and restore the lost heir to his throne. . . .

Lily Quench and the Black Mountains

In the Black Mountains there's nothing but snow, ice, and blizzards. But it's there that the magical blue lily grows, which can help Lily Quench and her friends stop the evil Black Count from invading their homeland.

With her friend Queen Dragon, Lily embarks on a perilous mission to bring the blue lily back to Ashby. Captured and imprisoned, then befriended by the count's son, Gordon, they flee to the eerie heights of Dragon's Downfall . . . the place where Lily and Queen Dragon must confront their greatest fear.